HAPPY KID!

GAIL GAUTHIER

G. P. Putnam's Sons

G. P. PUTNAM'S SONS

A division of Penguin Young Readers Group. Published by The Penguin Group.
Penguin Group (USA) Inc., 375 Hudson Street, New York, NY 10014, U.S.A.
Penguin Group (Canada), 90 Eglinton Avenue East, Suite 700, Toronto,
Ontario, Canada M4P 2Y3 (a division of Pearson Penguin Canada Inc.).
Penguin Books Ltd, 80 Strand, London WC2R 0RL, England.
Penguin Ireland, 25 St. Stephen's Green, Dublin 2, Ireland
(a division of Penguin Books Ltd.).
Penguin Group (Australia), 250 Camberwell Road, Camberwell, Victoria 3124, Australia
(a division of Pearson Australia Group Pty Ltd).
Penguin Books India Pvt Ltd, 11 Community Centre,
Panchsheel Park, New Delhi—110 017, India.
Penguin Group (NZ), Cnr Airborne and Rosedale Roads, Albany,
Auckland 1310, New Zealand (a division of Pearson New Zealand Ltd).
Penguin Books (South Africa) (Pty) Ltd, 24 Sturdee Avenue,
Rosebank, Johannesburg 2196, South Africa.
Penguin Books Ltd, Registered Offices: 80 Strand, London WC2R 0RL, England.

Published simultaneously in Canada.
Manufactured in China by South China Printing Co. Ltd.
Printed in the United States of America. Design by Marikka Tamura. Text set in Wilke.
Library of Congress Cataloging-in-Publication Data
Gauthier, Gail, 1953–
Happy kid! / Gail Gauthier. p. cm. Summary: After his mother bribes him into reading
a self-help book on how to form satisfying relationships and enjoy a happy life,
cynical eighth-grader Kyle finds there may be more to the book than he realized.
[1. Interpersonal relations—Fiction.   2. Self-help techniques—Fiction.
3. Middle schools—Fiction.   4. Schools—Fiction.]   I. Title.
PZ7.G23435 Hap 2006 [Fic]—dc22 2005003534 ISBN 0-399-24266-X
3 5 7 9 10 8 6 4 2

For Rob and Dan,
my sources of inspiration and information
and
thanks to everyone I train with
at Tae San Taekwondo Academy

CHAPTER 1

☹ ☹ ☺ ☹ ☹ ☹

"Kyle, Lauren, I have back to school presents!" Mom said as she handed us packages at dinner the night before my first day of seventh grade.

This can't be good, I thought.

I still hadn't recovered from my birthday, when Mom had given me a magazine subscription to encourage me to read, a pedometer to encourage me to exercise, and a museum pass to encourage me to be an old fart. A back to school present might be better, I supposed. But probably not.

My sister didn't think so, either.

"You open yours first," Lauren ordered.

"You're older. You should have to go first," I shot back.

Lauren sighed and opened her package. "Oh," she said as she studied the jewel case in her hand. "A computer program for preparing for the PSAT. What an unusual gift. How creative of you to think of it. I'll treasure it always. I—"

"You've probably said enough, Lauren," Dad said.

"What is the PSAT, anyway?" I asked.

"It's a test Lauren has to take this year as a practice for the Scholastic Aptitude Test she needs to take next year so she can go to college," Mom explained. "But, uh, you don't need to worry about that for a while."

"What? You said I don't have to take any more of those big, weird tests after I finish with the State Student Assessment Surveys in eighth grade," I reminded her.

"What I meant was that you wouldn't have to take the *SSASies* again after eighth grade," Mom said. "They stop giving them after that."

"Mom! You said—"

"Don't go off the deep end, Kyle," Dad said. "I'm trying to eat."

"I'm not going off the deep end!" I shouted.

"Hey, Kyle," Lauren said. "Remember when Mom told you you wouldn't have to have any more shots after your last physical? Well, guess what?"

I turned to my mother. "Is that true?"

"I meant you wouldn't have to have any more of *those* kinds of shots. But why are you getting all upset about shots and tests that you don't need to even be thinking about for years? Look! You haven't opened your present," Mom pointed out. "I saw it when I was shopping one day, and it just *screamed* your name."

"Open it up and get it over with, Kyle," Dad ordered. "I'm trying to eat."

I was backed into a corner with nothing to do but pick up

the package and rip the gift wrap off like I would a Band-Aid—quickly so the pain wouldn't be dragged out any longer than necessary.

"Happy Kid!" I read out loud when I saw the cover. *"A Young Person's Guide to Satisfying Relationships and a Happy and Meaning-Filled Life!"* I looked at my mother. *"This* screamed my name?"

"It was the strangest thing," Mom admitted. "I was cutting through the book department to get to men's underwear because your father needed new briefs. All of a sudden I noticed something shiny off to my right. It was the light reflecting off the gold lettering on that book. I saw the words *Happy Kid*, and your name popped into my mind. Right then and there I just knew that you could be a happy kid. I also, uh, well, I also suddenly experienced a feeling of great peace."

I dropped the book onto the table. "That's always a bad sign," I said.

Lauren agreed with me. "I know I'd be scared to death if I suddenly experienced a feeling of great peace while shopping for tightie-whities. Still, I have to admit it, Mom's right. That book is you all over, Kyle."

"Did you save the receipt?" I asked Mom. "Can I return it?"

"He took that well," Dad said as he helped himself to some pineapple chicken.

"Now, Kyle, what have you been taught about receiving gifts?" Mom said. "We aren't always going to get things we

3

like, but we have to remember the effort and thought be-hind them."

"Thank you for believing I'm such a reject I need a book on how to be happy," I said. "I really appreciate the thought."

"You are most welcome, I'm sure," Lauren replied as she popped a piece of pineapple into her mouth.

"Lauren, let your mother handle this," Dad said.

My mother is a child-and-family counselor. She handles everything. *Always.* For *everybody.* Friends, neighbors, people standing next to her in line at the grocery store—if they have a death in their family, a crazy relative, a kid in jail, work problems, car problems, pet problems, or plant problems, Mom will be all over it.

"If only she *could* handle this," Lauren sighed dramatically.

"A meaning-filled life?" I read again from the cover. "What is that, anyway? And I have satisfying relationships."

"You have relationships?" Lauren asked. "Since when?"

"Of course your brother has relationships," Mom said to Lauren. Then she looked toward me. "You just haven't . . . done anything . . . with them lately."

"Uh-oh. She must have noticed you spent the whole sum-mer alone in the living room watching disaster documen-taries," Lauren said. "And the Sci Fi Channel, of course."

She just can't shut up. It's like a curse or something with her.

"We care about your happiness," Mom told me, looking into my eyes with this sensitive, kind expression that must really creep out her clients. "You've changed since you started middle school last year. Even *before* the problem with . . . Mr. Kowsz . . . you weren't happy. You got upset so easily . . ."

"You started getting really hairy, too," Lauren broke in. "And you were only in sixth grade. What was with that?"

"Hey!" Dad said. "I'm *trying* to eat."

"Argh!"

"See what I mean about getting upset?" Mom went on. "You also saw less and less of your friends last year. You saw no one at all this summer. It's not good for you to spend so much time by yourself."

"I could have seen Jake Rogers," I replied. I was beginning to get a little angry because Mom and Lauren were dumping on me. "Would you have liked that? The last two weeks of school last year he wanted to be my new best buddy, you know. And you remember how he kept calling here the first few weeks of vacation?"

"He did seem awfully attracted to your notoriety, didn't he?" Mom admitted. Then a look of panic shot across her face as she realized she'd just admitted that I'd developed a little bit of a bad reputation at school the year before. "Not that you're notorious," she stammered. "And . . . and . . . I can't believe . . . um . . . that Jake Rogers is the only person you could have seen this *entire* summer. Not that there's anything . . . wrong . . . with the boy," Mom added quickly.

Sometimes I wonder just how well she does with the child-and-family-counseling thing.

"That's right, there's nothing wrong with Jake," Lauren agreed. "Except for the little business about being a future criminal. You know, I never understood that saying about people being known by the company they keep until you and Jake started getting so tight. You may not realize this, but he's not going to help your status at school at all."

"We're not tight!" I told her. "I don't want his company! He wants mine!"

"What about Lukie?" Mom asked me. "You guys were friends for years."

"Luke, Mom. Nobody says 'Lukie' now. We don't do things together anymore because we weren't in any classes together last year. We didn't even have the same lunch section. I didn't see him for most of sixth grade. You can't do things with someone you never see."

"He was in a different classroom, not on the other side of the world," Mom insisted.

"He might as well have been."

"Kyle, for the first time in your life you didn't have friends over for your birthday this summer!" Mom said.

"I was twelve, Mom. Give me a break."

"I had a *big* party for my twelfth birthday," Lauren recalled happily. "I had *boys* at my twelfth birthday party."

I spent part of my twelfth birthday with my grandmother. Oh my gosh. I am *such* a loser. A hairy loser.

"When you got your schedule from the school, did you even call any of your friends to find out if they have the same classes you do this year?" Mom asked.

6

I had a hard time imagining just which *friends* she was talking about. What with all the different classes we had last year at the middle school, I hadn't seen much of the people I'd known in grade school during the day. I had so much homework that I couldn't see much of anyone after school, either. You can't just call people you've hardly talked to since you left elementary school and hope they'll think you're *friends*. I wouldn't have been in good shape in that department even if there hadn't been the "problem with Mr. Kowsz," as Mom liked to call the worst thing that ever happened to me.

She was right, though. After the "problem," I did become notorious. Being famous for something no one wants to be famous for didn't suddenly make me a people magnet, either. Except for Jake Rogers, of course. He was the last straw. Once he started following me in the hall and hanging around me in the locker room before gym class (mine—he stopped going to his back in March), anyone who had been thinking about so much as asking if I'd been able to do last night's homework changed his mind.

A lot of people stared, though.

I didn't want to make my mother feel bad because I had no one to call, so instead of telling her that, I yelled, "Would you leave me alone!"

"No," Mom said. "I won't. Tell us what was wrong last year, and we'll try to help you fix it."

"Bert P. Trotts Middle School is the gateway to hell!" I shouted. "How are you going to fix that?"

"Yeah, I'd like to know that, too," Lauren said.

Mom turned so her back was toward Lauren. Which meant she was giving me all her attention. Yippee.

"Why is it the gateway to hell, sweetheart?" Mom asked me.

I decided I'd had enough of trying to be nice to my mother. I tried to change the subject and said, "I don't want to talk about this."

"Nah, he just wants to whine," Lauren announced.

"Lauren," Dad warned.

"I do not whine!" I shouted. "All the kids at Trotts spend all day every day being ordered around. 'Take this subject!' 'Listen to that teacher!' 'Run to your next class.' 'Read this book you don't like, do this homework you don't understand, sit with these kids you don't know.' 'Do this. And this. And this.' It never lets up. Not for a minute. 'You got your homework done? Great! Here's some more.' 'And what do you think about what happened in the book we're reading? Really? Well, you're *wrong!*' "

"Wait until you get out in the work world," Dad told me, man-to-man. "You'll *wish* you were back at the gateway to hell."

"Honey," Mom said to me, "we know the new accelerated English and social studies classes you took last year were tons of work. I felt just terrible when you had to drop out of Boy Scouts because you didn't have time for the meetings. And then there was the . . . well, the problem with Mr.

Kowsz . . . in June. But you need to understand, sweetheart, that there are two responses to difficulty. One is positive and one is negative. You've become very negative and defensive, and we'd like to help you become positive and accepting. We'd like to help you—"

I couldn't listen to any more of that stuff. "I am not negative!" I exclaimed.

"Not negative?" Lauren repeated, laughing. "Kyle, your glass isn't just half empty . . . it's broken and the water has spilled all over the floor."

I could have added that the water was muddy and full of bacteria, but I didn't. I have a much sunnier personality than I get credit for.

Mom either smiled or gritted her teeth at me. "You always look for the worst in every situation, Kyle. And then you get all upset about it. It's as if you don't know how to do anything else anymore. We're worried about your happiness. Your father and I think it's time for you to start fresh."

Oh, yeah, sure, like Dad had anything to do with any of this.

"Kyle, read this book," Mom insisted. "It could change your life."

"Is it part of a trilogy?" Lauren asked. "Because one book is not going to be anywhere near enough to fix what's wrong with him."

"*You'd* need an entire set of encyclopedias," I shot back.

"Read the damn book, Kyle," Dad said. "At worst it will be

a waste of time. And at best my ulcer will shrink up because there won't be squabbling at the dinner table anymore."

"Dad, you do not have an ulcer," Lauren groaned.

Dad corrected her. "No one has been able to *find* my ulcer. But it is there. And it's growing. Terrorist threats, unemployment, new diseases, and now two adolescents living in the same house with me. Why I'm not on a liquid diet by now is a mystery to me."

My father isn't exactly what I'd describe as positive and accepting. Why doesn't Mom ever jump on him?

"I'm not reading that book," I announced. "You can't make me."

"I'll pay you a dollar for every chapter you read," Mom suddenly offered.

Lauren gasped—one of those big fake ones that involve a huge, noisy sucking-in of air. She's tall and thin, and she usually wears her dark hair in a ponytail or pinned up on the back of her head with a clip. With her hair up you really notice her gray eyes popping open when she's surprised.

I look just like her except I don't have breasts.

Actually, she doesn't, either.

"You're going to bribe him?" Lauren asked.

"It's behavior modification," Mom said grimly. "Read a chapter, get a reward."

"And that's different from bribery because . . . ?"

I picked the book up and looked it over. It was pretty big.

"Not worth it," I said.

"Kyle, you idiot," Lauren exclaimed. "You only get seven

dollars a week for allowance. If you read a chapter a day, you'll double your income. How long are the chapters? They're only a page long! Give me that book. For a dollar a page, *I'll* read it."

"No," I said, pulling the book away from her. "It's mine."

CHAPTER 2

☹ 😐 ☺ 😐 ☹ 😐

When I woke up on the first day of seventh grade, I wanted only three things from life. I wanted to keep people from staring at me and whispering. I wanted to get my name off any school lists of students who were likely to snap and go violent. And I wanted to buy one of the bacon, egg, and cheese bagels the Bert P. Trotts Middle School lunch ladies sell before first-period classes start.

I thought I had a chance for the first two items on my list if I could just be quiet and keep people from noticing me for, say, six or seven months, so everyone would forget I'd ever existed. I didn't have a clue how I could get the third item because, unfortunately, bacon, egg, and cheese bagels aren't handed out free in the hallways. It was no use hitting up my mother for money because she couldn't understand why we didn't love the lame food she made for us at home. I could probably find seventy-five cents in change on the floor of my bedroom, but I needed a dollar and a half. Where would I get the rest of it?

I rolled over onto my side and moaned. Then I noticed something shiny off to my right. A ray of sunlight was reflecting off some gold lettering. I saw the words *Happy Kid* peeking out from under the shirt I'd been wearing the day before. Suddenly I experienced a feeling of great peace.

That bacon, egg, and cheese bagel was mine.

The book felt as if no one had ever even opened the cover, because the binding was incredibly stiff. But when I managed to pry a few pages apart, I found I was looking at a chapter that was only a paragraph long. That was very convenient since it just happened to be all I wanted to read.

It All Begins with Hello!

Building great relationships begins with the word "hello"! You can't build a satisfying relationship with someone if you won't even open your mouth. You have to let people know you're there! Say hello to those strangers you've been sitting next to for years. Once you've started talking, it's easy to keep talking. Compliment someone on a new outfit. Pass on something you've read in the paper. Make a point every day to speak to the people around you. Before long, you'll be doing it without even thinking!

As I slammed the book shut, I was overwhelmed with a powerful emotion. It was embarrassment for my mother. I hoped no one our family knew had seen her buying the sappy thing. Then I got over it, jumped to my feet, and headed out to the kitchen.

"I won't be needing that," I told Mom, who was slicing grapefruit. She had already poured out two bowls of a cold cereal that had been invented someplace in Scandinavia where all the healthiest and worst-tasting breakfast food comes from. "I'm getting a bacon, egg, and cheese bagel this morning. Could I have a dollar?"

Mom kept right on working away over that grapefruit and said, "You know I'm not paying for you to kill yourself with that stuff."

"But you are paying me to read that book you got me."

Mom stopped what she was doing and slowly turned around. Her face looked as if it might explode. Then she calmed down enough to just look sly and confused. I knew she was wondering how to find out if I'd really read a chapter without accusing me of lying. I decided to give her a break and get my dollar a little faster. I was not going to miss the bus that day and risk getting to school late so everyone would gawk at me while I was walking into class.

"*Hello*, Mom," I said cheerfully. "Lovely pair of black corduroys you're wearing. I particularly like the way they whistle when your legs rub together while you're walking."

"That wasn't in the first chapter," Mom said as the telephone started to ring.

"It was in whatever chapter I happened to find. I read a chapter, I get a dollar. That's what you said," I reminded her. Then I picked up the phone.

"Put your TV on!" a voice ordered from the other end of the line. "They're changing the colors for the terrorist alerts!"

14

"Why, *hello*, Nana dear," I replied, holding out my open hand to my mother. "Have you read the paper already this morning, or were you just watching the news?"

"Kyle? Is that you? Did I get a wrong number?"

"Great book, Mom," I said. "I say hello to my own nana, and she doesn't recognize me."

"Take a dollar out of my wallet," Mom sighed as she took the receiver from me.

I carried my dollar up the stairs toward my room, pausing just long enough to pound on the bathroom door as I passed it and shout, "*Hello?* That bathroom is supposed to be for both of us!"

"Go use Mom's!"

I'd had to use my mother's bathroom in the mornings ever since I got out of elementary school and had to take the same bus as my sister. We have two bathrooms for four people. I may be bad at math, but even I can figure out that you would never divide four by two and come up with an answer that involved putting one person in one bathroom and three in another. So I try to remind Lauren of the unfairness of that situation whenever I think of it.

I've had appliances glued to the roof of my mouth to correct a cross bite twice (because *of course* it didn't work the first time) and tiny chains attached to impacted second teeth so they could be pulled down out of my gums. I've had braces with elastic bands for nearly three years now. You wouldn't think a little tiny rubber band would be capable of causing the kind of ache and sometimes real pain that these things are

15

able to cause. And the crud that gets on the brackets on my teeth whenever I forget to be careful about what I eat takes more than a little time to pick off. So I think it just stands to reason that I should be able to get into my own bathroom where all my toothbrushes, floss, wax, and dental mirrors are stored.

Wait! What was I thinking? Of course taking a shower and trying out different ways to put your hair up into a ponytail are more important than something petty like *pain and suffering.*

I grabbed some clothes and headed off to my parents' bedroom at the other end of the hall. Once I was in their room, I tiptoed past the lump under the covers on the bed. I stopped and looked at it, thinking, He's asleep. It's not necessary to speak to a sleeping person. Not only is it not necessary, it's mean. Why would I—

Then, right in the middle of a thought, I said, "*Hello,* Dad."

Dad raised his head up a little bit off the pillow and tried to open his eyes.

"What's wrong?" he said groggily. "Smoke alarm go off? Fire? Somebody sick?"

"I just said hello," I repeated, feeling a little bit guilty for shaking him up like that. "Go back to sleep."

"Did I hear the phone ringing? At this hour? Is somebody dead?" Dad asked.

"Your mother called."

"What does she want?" he groaned as he started to stretch for the telephone by the bed.

"She wanted us to know that the Homeland Security dude was changing the colors for the terrorist alert."

"Up or down?"

"She didn't say."

Dad collapsed back onto his pillow as I went on to the bathroom.

"It must be up," he muttered. "She never calls with good news."

"Have a good day," Mom called when we went out the front door a while later.

As if telling me to have a good day will make it happen. My mother lives in a fantasy world.

Our driver, who had pretended she didn't know me for the last two weeks of sixth grade, was all smiles when I got on the bus, as if she figured that over the summer I'd forgotten all about her part in the "problem with Mr. Kowsz." Well, if the newspaper hadn't been full of stories about me until nearly the Fourth of July, maybe I would have. I started to move by her as fast as I could.

But at the last minute I suddenly gave her a big "hello." Then I kept saying "hello, hello, hello" to everyone as I went down the aisle. I didn't stop until Lauren, who was right behind me, slapped the side of my head and told me to stop being a jerk.

I found an empty seat and tried to disappear into it. What had I been thinking? Nothing. I hadn't been thinking anything at all. Because never, ever would I have thought to say hello to a whole bunch of people. Some of the kids on that bus were high school kids I didn't even know. Some of them I didn't even like. You don't keep people from noticing you by saying hello to them.

I pulled the copy of *Killer Hurricanes, Tornadoes, and Tsunamis* that my father had given me for my birthday out of my backpack and concentrated on making people forget I existed by pretending to read.

The bus left us off in front of two large brick buildings that shared an enormous parking lot. We split up on the sidewalk, with the middle-schoolers heading over to Trotts and the high school students walking over to their school. From the curb I could see our principal, Mr. Alldredge, standing by the front door. With his black hair and mustache (both dyed, according to Lauren) and very square, toothy smile, he looked like Saddam Hussein, which helped to explain why he wasn't the most beloved adult at school. I tried to act as if I didn't know he was watching me as I walked by him.

By the time I was safely inside, I was starving. I could practically taste that bacon, egg, and cheese as I entered the building and headed right for the cafeteria. I could feel its greasiness in my mouth. I could see it glistening in my hand. What I couldn't do was smell it. When I reached the cafeteria door, I found out why.

BREAKFIST SERVISE BEGINS AGAIN NEXT WEEK.

The lunch ladies will never win any spelling bees. But they can make a bagel sandwich worth going to war for.

18

"No!" I wailed, letting my backpack slide slowly to the floor.

The hallway was crowded with kids who didn't know where they were going and a few people bumped into me while I stood there hoping none of them had noticed me shouting. Then I just had this feeling that there was someone behind me. Someone who ought to be moving but wasn't. I looked over my shoulder.

Mr. Kowsz, the tallest, skinniest, oldest tech ed teacher in the school, maybe the state, was standing there staring right back at me. He looked just the way he did the year before. Except for the cast on his left foot. That was different.

"Moo" Kowsz was famous for two things: knowing way less about technology than the worst salesperson Radio Shack ever employed, and patrolling the halls of Bert P. Trotts looking for kids gone bad.

The last time he spoke to me was about a week and a half before school got out. He had called me over to one side of the room during class, slapped me on the back, laughed, and said, "Well, who could have predicted that, huh? Misunderstandings happen. Let's just move on and forget it."

"Move on and forget it?" I'd shouted, right in front of all the other students. "Everybody's treating me like a mass murderer who was caught just in the nick of time! Everybody saw my picture in the paper! Everybody's talking about me and looking at me! How am I supposed to forget anything?"

The room had gotten very quiet, and everyone stared at me—pretty much the way they'd have stared at me if I *were* a mass murderer who had been caught just in the nick of time.

Technology education class was really awkward after that.

And here was ol' Moo on my first day of seventh grade opening his mouth to say something to me. I didn't want anyone to see us together in the hallway and wonder what we were talking about. I decided I had to get out of there as fast as I could. So what did I do to make that happen? I sputtered, "Hello." It just came rolling right out of my mouth.

He hadn't been expecting that. His head snapped back and down at the same time, which made his mouth shut. I saw my chance and bent to pick up my backpack. Fortunately, by the time I was standing up again, Mr. Kowsz had turned his head and was sniffing.

"Somebody's smoking already," he snapped and took off toward the nearest bathroom.

I swear, I didn't smell a thing.

I went to look for my advisory classroom. When I found it, the teacher there poked her head full of dark roots and bleached blond hair up over the top of a newspaper as I entered the room. She had a line of dark hair on her upper lip, too. (Not that there's anything wrong with having a hairy lip. *I'd* never criticize someone for being hairy.) According to my schedule, this was Mrs. Haag.

"Hello," I said. I didn't know the word was coming until I heard my voice saying it. I had no time to even try to stop it.

Mrs. Haag dropped her newspaper and looked at me. I

could tell not many people said hello to her. She definitely wasn't used to it.

"And you are?" she asked me.

I almost groaned out loud, but I did manage to catch that. If I'd just walked into the classroom and sat down, she would have been able to ignore me until it was time to take attendance. Then she would have just read my name, grunted when I said "here," and gone on to the next person. But oh, no, I had to say "hello." Now this Mrs. Haag felt pressured to keep the conversation going.

"Kyle Rideau," I whispered.

"What was that?" she asked.

"Kyle Rideau," I snapped back.

There was a little lull in the buzz of conversation, and, sure enough, all the students in the room were watching me.

"Oh, I know who you are," Mrs. Haag said.

I looked down at the floor and said, "Yeah, that's me."

"Sure. I think I had your sister when she was here. Her name was Laura, right?"

"Lauren."

"Oh, yes. She was an . . . interesting . . . girl."

I couldn't believe my luck. Mrs. Haag only knew me as Lauren's brother. Never had I been so happy that my sister was an . . . interesting . . . girl. Mrs. Haag was even laughing! So I started to laugh, too.

Then she said, "So it was Lauren Rideau's little brother who got into all that trouble last spring. I never made the connection."

The laughing pretty much stopped after that.

"I didn't get into all that much trouble," I said in a low voice I hoped only she would hear.

"You would have preferred getting into more?"

Of course I wouldn't have! I didn't want to get into some big discussion about it, either. I didn't think I was going to be able to avoid it, but then I was saved by, of all people, Melissa Esposito. She came into the room at just that moment, and she can't pass a teacher without stopping to suck up. I took off while good old dependable Melissa distracted Mrs. Haag by informing her that she was going to be in Mrs. Haag's health and living class and asking just what would they be covering in class this year. And doing a great job of sounding as if she really cared.

If I hadn't been so busy making my getaway, I would have been upset about Melissa being in my advisory. I would have also given some thought to how she must have grown two bra sizes over the summer. Her hips looked as if they'd been doing some growing, too. Now she had big curves to match her big brown eyes and her big brown braid. And her big mouth. She has an opinion on almost any subject that comes up and feels the whole world deserves to know what she thinks.

I saw a desk I wanted at the back of the room. To reach it, I had to pass Jamie Lombardi and Beth Pritchard, these popular girls who nobody really likes. It was going to be a treat spending an extra eight minutes a day with them all year, too.

"I had to spend, like, all Labor Day with my grandparents and my aunt," Beth said.

"Like, why?" Jamie asked Beth.

"My grandfather has been in the hospital, like, four times this year. It is, like, so gross," Beth complained.

"Oh! Oh!" Jamie exclaimed. "I know something grosser than that! I had to, like, go to a funeral!"

They both stopped talking when I walked between them. Jamie leaned across the aisle toward Beth and gasped, "Kyle Rideau is, like, in our advisory." As if, like, Beth couldn't figure that out for herself.

Maybe she couldn't.

"Hello," I said as I settled into the seat behind Jamie. By that point, I wasn't even surprised to hear myself say it.

They were, though. They were both so stunned that I had said something to them that they shut up for a whole second or two. Then they looked at each other and giggled.

"Did you notice the article in the paper yesterday about the high rate of skin cancer in Australia?" I asked.

Jamie and Beth looked at each other again. I'm guessing neither one of them had ever read a newspaper in her entire life. Not even the comics.

"Gross!" they both squealed.

That was the last they had to say about me because they got really involved in a discussion about the birthday present they'd bought for Melissa and whether or not they should give it to her or keep it and buy something else. That left me free to look around for Luke Slocum or maybe someone I used to sit next to in one of my classes last year. But the only people I knew were a couple of kids from my gym class I'd hoped never to see again.

Math was my first class after advisory. Math is not my strongest subject, and the longer I study it, the worse I get. There are some kids at Trotts who take pre-algebra in seventh grade. I am not one of them.

"Hello, Mr. Pierce," I said without even thinking about it as I walked by the math teacher's desk. A moment or two later, though, I did realize what I'd done. I looked over my shoulder to see if I could catch Mr. Pierce's reaction.

He seemed confused. He couldn't figure out who had spoken to him. He was standing hunched over his book and looking all around the room. I wondered if maybe I ought to tell him I was the one who had said hello, but I couldn't think of any way to do it that wouldn't make everyone look at me. So I just headed for an empty seat.

Then from behind me I heard a familiar voice saying to Mr. Pierce, "Yeah, hello, Mr. . . . um . . . whoever the hell you are." I looked back toward the front of the classroom and saw Jake Rogers walking down the aisle right behind me, laughing his head off. He raised his arm to high-five me and gasped, "Hey, Kyle! My man!"

Jake Rogers is enormous, and he always has been. He's always looked way older than he is. Now he looks as if he's just escaped from a men's prison. He may not actually be able to beat the crap out of everyone—student or adult—at Trotts, but he sure looks as if he could.

I didn't want to be the one who had to tell Jake that nobody high-fives anymore. But there I was with his arm hovering over me while everyone in the room noticed me. And noticed me with him. My new math teacher watched us as if he could tell we were going to be the two troublemakers who would make the next school year the unhappiest of his life. Beth Pritchard had followed me from advisory, and she was watching, too, and looking not at all surprised to see Jake acting so friendly toward me. In fact, no one seemed to think it was unusual for Jake Rogers and Kyle Rideau to be greeting each other in the middle of the math classroom.

To the whole school Jake and I were two of a kind.

Instead of slapping Jake's hand, I just brought my own up, waved it at him, and said, "Hello?"

CHAPTER 3

☹ 🙂 🙂 😐 ☹ 😐

First period hadn't even started and it already looked as if there was a good chance seventh grade was going to go pretty much the way sixth grade did.

And sixth grade had been the worst year of my life.

Bert P. Trotts is the only middle school in our town, so all the kids from all *three* of the elementary schools end up there, all mixed together. That meant I'd never met two-thirds of the kids in my grade. Still, you'd think that just by chance there'd be some familiar faces in at least one of the seven classes I had each day. But, no, I was lucky if I knew anyone at all in any of them. Even my lunch section seemed to be loaded with kids from those other schools.

In my opinion, meeting new people is not everything it's cracked up to be. Especially if you are accidentally placed in accelerated English and social studies classes the way I was in sixth grade. Those classes were filled with new people, like Melissa Esposito, who were smarter and faster than I was. Fortunately, I was so busy trying to do my accelerated homework in a smarter and faster way that I didn't have a lot of time to feel bad about how poorly the meeting-new-people thing was going.

I also threw up for three days during the April break.

But as bad as sixth grade was, I almost got through it. I had only a couple of weeks left to go before summer vacation. Then things got a lot worse.

And I'm not talking about final exams.

I was on the bus on my way home from school one afternoon in June. The seat across from me emptied out after one of the stops, so I moved my backpack onto it. I just wanted a little more room. As my backpack made the trip from one seat to another, a screwdriver fell out onto the floor. So, of course, I had to bend down to pick it up. The bus driver heard the screwdriver hit the floor. She looked up into the mirror that gives her a view of her passengers just in time to see me with it in my hand as I used the cushion of the seat in front of me to pull myself back up. The girl sitting there started screeching because she thought I wanted to sit with her, which was absolutely not true. I had an entire seat to myself. Why would I want to sit with a screecher? She was kind of flattering herself.

The next thing I knew, the driver was turning the bus around and heading in the opposite direction.

We thought we were being kidnapped, and some of the older girls used their cell phones to call their boyfriends to tell them they loved them. (My mother was so P.O.'ed when she found out Lauren had called her new boyfriend, Jared, instead of her.) One of the boyfriends called the police, and a state trooper pulled up behind us. He flashed his lights, and the bus driver flashed hers back at him. As it turned out, she was just headed back to the school. But she didn't let us out once she got there. Instead she sat in her seat with the door closed until the trooper, who had followed us all the way there, got out of his car and was standing at the bottom of the bus steps. Then she opened the door and told him, "Fourth seat on the left. Weapon."

Coincidentally, I was sitting in the fourth seat on the left. I was so shocked when I heard her say those words that I just stayed there and watched as this big guy with tall leather boots and dark glasses came down the aisle and stopped next to me.

I was still holding the screwdriver in my hand because I had been too shook up to put it back in my backpack. Plus, I was kind of confused about how it had fallen out, not knowing that, after having been jammed point-down in the pack since second period, the screwdriver had worn a hole in the bottom.

"Come on, son," the officer said. "You don't want to hurt anybody with that thing."

I looked down at the screwdriver. "This? This is a Father's Day present. For my dad."

He grabbed me by the shoulder and dragged me away. Lauren swears that she tried to get off the bus to help me, but the driver wouldn't let anyone leave. A likely story. I was sitting in the back of the police cruiser as the bus drove away again, and I could see Lauren through one of the back windows with her cell phone pressed to her ear and her mouth moving a mile a minute. She didn't even wave.

The state trooper didn't want to leave me alone in his car while he went into the school to get the principal, so he radioed his dispatcher for help. Sitting in a police cruiser with a cop is nowhere near as cool as you'd think. Parents kept driving up to the school to pick up kids who had stayed late. I could see all the moms and dads and their kids staring through the windows, trying to see who'd been caught.

Finally, the principal came out, and the officer showed him the screwdriver. I thought, Thank goodness. Mr. Alldredge will explain everything. After all, I had made the screwdriver in tech ed class. It was an assignment. Nobody goes to jail for a school assignment.

Mr. Alldredge looked at the screwdriver, looked at me, and said, "Why don't we all go into my office."

I thought, Okay, he'll explain everything in his office.

First, though, we made our own little parade as we walked through the school lobby: the principal, the uniformed state trooper, and me. And wouldn't you know it, Melissa Esposito and the rest of the girls' track team were posing with their trophy for a photographer from our local newspaper, *The Daily Report*.

Melissa already thought I was an idiot, anyway, and she was very obvious about it. So I guessed having her see me hauled through the school wasn't going to make things any worse than they already were.

But standing right next to Melissa was Chelsea Donahue. Chelsea was the most fantastic girl in the sixth grade. She was smart and cool, had long, blond hair, and was nearly as tall as I was. She was the first girl you noticed in any group. Chelsea was also in my accelerated classes. If she thought I was an idiot, she wasn't obvious about it. Though we'd never had a conversation or even really spoken, we did do oral reports on the same book once.

I hoped she thought the state trooper was my father.

"So, Kyle, what were you doing with the screwdriver?" Mr. Alldredge asked as he slipped behind his desk once we were in his office.

"I was taking it home."

"Why did you bring it to school in the first place?"

"I didn't. I made it here at school. We made them in tech ed. Mr. Kowsz will tell you."

Mr. Alldredge gave me a "you are such a liar" smile. "That's not part of the tech ed curriculum. Are you trying to tell me that *Mr. Kowsz* did something with his class that was not in the curriculum? Mr. Kowsz never breaks rules," he said, sounding as if that was a bad thing. "Mr. Kowsz goes out of his way to enforce them."

I froze for a while. My class was supposed to have spent the week before in the computer lab learning how to make spreadsheets. But Mr. Kowsz couldn't even use e-mail. So whenever we went to the computer lab, he had one of the kids in the class figure out the lesson plan and show the others how to do it.

But who wants to make spreadsheets? So we all said, "Spread *what*?" Then, instead of skipping ahead to making wrought-iron candlesticks (which is *technology* education how?), Mr. Kowsz had us make screwdrivers so we wouldn't get ahead of the other tech ed classes.

If only he had just let us surf the Net that week the way we'd suggested.

Mr. Alldredge leaned forward and started tapping away at a keyboard. He looked at the monitor, then he looked at me. Then he looked at the monitor again.

"Hmmm. Kyle, I don't see your name coming up on any of our school clubs or events. You don't do any sports?" Mr. Alldredge asked.

"No."

"Drama Club? Newspaper? Peer Helpers?"

"Ah . . . no."

Mr. Alldredge looked over at the state trooper. I read the CNN website. I knew what he was driving at with all those questions. All your most famous kid criminals steer clear of after-school activities. As bad as being escorted through the parking lot and school by a state trooper had been, I had a feeling things were going to get much, much worse.

"Which one of your parents should we call?" Mr. Alldredge asked.

Well, *there* was a question I could spend an hour or more trying to answer. Here I was, sitting in the principal's office with a state trooper. Did I want my mother or my father to be the first to hear the news?

"You could just ask Mr. Kowsz," I suggested. "He'll tell you that I made the screwdriver in class."

Mr. Alldredge's big, fuzzy eyebrows shot up. "You don't want us to call your parents? Why doesn't that surprise me?"

"Call my father," I sighed. "My mother sees clients all day long and will have trouble getting away. My father is a systems analyst. No one knows what he does, anyway, and it won't matter if he leaves his office."

Mr. Alldredge sent me to the reception area to wait. The trooper came out and stood by the doorway that led to the hall, in case I tried to make a run for it. Then Mr. Alldredge came out and went over to some equipment in a corner behind the secretaries. In a moment I heard his voice calling Mr. Kowsz's name on the intercom. Maybe, I thought, this could all be cleared up before Dad gets here, and we can just go home.

But Mr. Kowsz didn't show up.

He still wasn't there when Jake Rogers got out of detention. Jake was someone I actually had gone to elementary school with. I'd spent most of those years trying to stay out of his way, so he wasn't one of the familiar faces I'd been hoping to see in my classes when I arrived at the middle school back in September. I wasn't happy to see him just then, either. Jake knew me well enough to seem surprised to see me sitting next to a state trooper as he walked past the office. Surprised and impressed. His eyes bulged out of his head, and his mouth gaped open. Then he pointed one fat, scaly finger at me while he gave me the thumbs-up sign with his other hand.

I had impressed Jake Rogers. That gave me something to think about while I continued to wait for Mr. Kowsz and my father.

"Kyle!" Dad exclaimed when he arrived and came rushing toward me. "What happened?"

"I was bringing this thing home that we made in tech ed, and all of a sudden the bus driver took us back to the school and a trooper came onto the bus and—"

Mr. Alldredge suddenly appeared. "Why don't you wait until we're in my office," he suggested. "We'll all be more comfortable there."

I didn't think that was very likely.

"Mr. Rideau, were you aware that Kyle brought a screwdriver to school today?" Mr. Alldredge asked after we'd all sat down across from his desk.

"What were you doing with a screwdriver?" Dad asked me. "I've never even seen you use one."

"I did not bring a screwdriver to school. I made it in technology education," I explained.

Dad's head swung back toward the principal.

"There are no units in the technology education curriculum on making screwdrivers or any other kind of tool," Mr. Alldredge said.

"Mr. Kowsz will tell you," I insisted. "There are sixteen other kids in the class. Any of them will tell you, too."

"Mr. Kowsz leaves the building early a couple of days a week. We just got in touch with him on his cell phone, so it will be a few minutes before he gets back here," Mr. Alldredge told us.

The state trooper sighed and stretched his legs out in front of him. I think he was getting bored.

"So is it a screwdriver he made himself?" Dad asked Mr. Alldredge.

Mr. Alldredge picked it up off his desk to show him.

"Oh, wow. You made that, Kyle?" Dad said. "Very nice."

"That screwdriver is a contraband item under Section Three, Subsection Four, of the Disciplinary Section of the *Bert P. Trotts Student-Parent Handbook*." Mr. Alldredge stopped speaking long enough to hold up a form with signatures on it. "You received a copy of the handbook in September and returned this form stating that you had read it. Both you and Kyle signed it. That is your signature, isn't it?"

"Oh, yes. I actually . . . remember . . . signing that form."

He remembered signing the form, but I guessed he didn't remember reading the handbook. The thing is over sixty pages long, with no pictures and small print. Dad flipped through it when I brought it home and said, "I think I'll just skim this."

Mr. Alldredge had read every word, though. He opened the book up.

"Section Three: Activities Leading to Suspension, Expulsion, or Legal Action. Subsection Four: Possession of any weapon, including but not limited to deadly weapons,

34

firearms, whether loaded or unloaded, knives, whether sharpened or not, explosive devices, whether functional or not, blackjacks, maces, brass knuckles, grappling hooks, dart guns, crossbows, or *any other dangerous object*."

Mr. Alldredge dropped the handbook onto his desk and looked up at us. "Do you have any idea how dangerous a screwdriver can be?"

"Oh, yeah. Two of the guys were sword fighting with their screwdrivers in class. I was sitting there waiting for an eye to come flying out at me. Nothing happened, though," I assured him.

"Why was he asked to make something so dangerous in class?" Dad asked.

Mr. Alldredge shook his head. "He wasn't."

"It's clearly a handmade tool," Dad pointed out. "He didn't make it at home. Except for studying, all he does is hole up in front of the computer or the television. He doesn't go out, so he couldn't have made it somewhere else."

At that point I began to wonder if Dad should stop trying to help.

"He had to have made it here," he continued. "It seems unreasonable to me to ask him to make something and then call in the police when he tries to bring it home. What was he supposed to do with it?"

That was better.

"Kyle, why were you holding the screwdriver in your hand on the bus?" the state trooper broke in. "What were you going to do with it?"

35

"It fell out of my backpack," I explained. "And then the bus driver took off—we thought she was kidnapping us, you know—and I just sat there with it. I didn't think to try to put it away."

As the trooper went to pick my backpack up off the floor next to Mr. Alldredge's desk, Mr. Kowsz knocked on the door and entered the office.

"I'm sorry to have to call you back to school, but this young man was caught with a weapon, which he claims he made in your second-period class," Mr. Alldredge said.

"A weapon? We don't make weapons in second period," Mr. Kowsz said as he was sitting down. As if maybe "we" made them in another period.

"Do you make screwdrivers?" Dad asked.

Mr. Kowsz blinked. He blinked again. Then he nodded his head once. "I try to do a hands-on technical design activity-related project at this time of year that interfaces with our exploration of manufacturing and construction technology."

Mr. Alldredge and the state trooper just stared at him, but my father smiled and said, "Ah. Screwdrivers."

"The kids are supposed to use them for Father's Day presents," Mr. Kowsz continued. He gave me this really serious look. "Not for weapons."

The state trooper shoved the bottom of my backpack up for everyone to see. "There's a hole in the bottom of this thing," he pointed out. "The screwdriver just slipped through it."

There was a pause while everyone thought about that.

"So, we're agreed that Kyle hasn't done anything wrong?" Dad finally asked, standing up.

"I agree," I said.

The principal did, too. He wasn't so sure about Mr. Kowsz, though. He made Mr. Kowsz stay after the rest of us left. He said they had something to discuss.

Dad and I walked out to the parking lot with the state trooper.

"I cannot come back to school tomorrow," I said after we left the trooper at his cruiser and headed on to our car. "Everyone will know."

"What will they know? That the principal made a fool of himself over a screwdriver?" Dad asked.

"They'll know the principal and the state police—the bus driver, even!—thought I was some kind of weirdo who goes around attacking people with hand tools! I've never even been in a fight. I've never been in any trouble at all. But everyone was willing to believe I was a maniac armed with a screwdriver."

"That's not your fault," Dad said.

"It's not my fault, but I was the one who was blamed," I reminded him. Had he already forgotten where we'd just been? "All kinds of people saw me in that state trooper's car. Parents saw me! Kids from my classes saw me with the state trooper and the principal. You know what they're thinking?"

"No, I don't, Kyle. And neither do you."

"Yes, I do! They're thinking Kyle Rideau must be the kind of guy people suspect when there's trouble. They're thinking

I would never have been in that cruiser if there wasn't a *reason*. Why did that bus driver think I would use a screwdriver as a weapon? She's known me all year. Mom made me give her a Christmas present. I gave her cookies, and look what she did to me!"

Right in the middle of the parking lot Dad stopped and hugged me. "She was just scared," he said.

"Of me? She was scared of me?" I said into his shoulder.

"She was just scared, period. And you just happened to be there. That's all it was. It's all over now."

I should have given him a shove or something because we were both way too old for a father-son hug. But a hug from your father reminds you of all those times you broke your best toy and your dad said, "Don't worry. I can fix it. Everything will be okay." And then everything was. That hug out in the parking lot convinced me that what had happened really was over and done with.

Boy, was I wrong.

When I went back to school the next day, everybody knew. And if anyone didn't know, they found out by last period. Because instead of a shot of the girls' track team, the next day's *Daily Report* carried a blurry picture of me being hugged by my daddy in the Trotts parking lot. "Unidentified student is comforted by his father after bus incident," the caption read because, though reporters can get basic information about police investigations since they are part of the public record, they can't print the names of people under eighteen without their parents' permission. So all the article said was that the student in the photo was questioned by state police regarding possession of a weapon on a bus filled with middle- and high-school students. That was enough.

Jamie Lombardi and Beth Pritchard don't read the newspaper, but they didn't need to. An amazingly large number of people do, and they told everyone else. Melissa Esposito actually brought that morning's paper to school with her that day. My teachers must have been passing a copy around in the faculty lounge because they were all being extra nice to me, as if they were afraid I'd snap and start twitching right in front of them. My afternoon classes were very, very quiet and a path magically cleared for me in every hallway.

Later in the week there was a newspaper story about the PTO holding a special meeting on school violence because of a recent act of aggression by "an unidentified student." Then came a story about the school board requesting an inquiry because of a confrontation on a bus with "an unidentified student." One day the paper carried an interview with Mr. Alldredge in which he said he couldn't comment on this incident because it would violate the "unidentified student's" privacy. As if I had any left. I swear, for weeks the newspapers were full of articles about an "unidentified student" who was always described as having been involved in some kind of "assault" or "attack."

My mother saved them for her scrapbook.

None of this would have happened if it hadn't been for Mr. Kowsz. He was the one who came up with the lame screwdriver assignment because he can barely figure out how to turn on the computers in his classroom. Did anybody write articles for the newspaper about him? He's well over the age of eighteen. The newspaper could have published his name without asking his parents. They're probably dead, anyway. But no, no one wrote a word about how the principal and the school superintendent called Mr. Kowsz in for a meeting and told him he'd have to have his lesson plans checked every morning at the office for the rest of the year to make sure he was teaching what he was supposed to. They also said he'd have to get some computer training, which I think they should have thought of a long time ago. It wasn't as if they were letting him get by because they liked him. Both Mr. Alldredge and the school superintendent are supposed to have been mad at Mr. Kowsz for a couple of years because he made a big fuss about a gym teacher he caught swearing at a kid.

How did I know all this if I didn't read it in the paper? I heard it from Jake Rogers, of course. Jake always knows all kinds of things about the teachers because he listens to as much as he can when he's sent to the office. And he's sent there all the time. Not often enough that June, as far as I was concerned. When Jake wasn't in the office those last couple weeks of school, he was sticking to me like a boil, telling me all about the news he had picked up in the office and the creepy friends he'd made while serving detention. He thought I was some kind of hero or something because, as awful as he is, he had never done anything that involved the police.

I couldn't believe I said hello to him before first period on the first day of seventh grade and that my new math teacher and Beth Pritchard and I don't know how many other people had seen me do it. I couldn't understand how it happened because I really was not a "hello" kind of guy.

CHAPTER 4

☹ 😐 🙂 😐 ☹ 😐

Jake Rogers has been known to steal money from smaller kids, knock people off their feet by jerking on their backpacks, kick in lockers so they can't be opened anymore, and rip apart other kids' textbooks so they have to pay fines. His grades were so bad in sixth grade that he had to go to summer school to repeat some of his courses. Lauren heard he had a great time there. I'm guessing no one else did.

So when he thought my saying hello to Mr. Pierce was just so incredibly funny, that was a good thing. Because if Jake's laughing, he's not doing something a whole lot worse. But who wants everyone to know he's the kind of guy Jake Rogers thinks is funny?

Unfortunately, by the time Jake got through laughing and saying hello to Beth and some of the other girls—and sitting next to me—everyone knew.

Our homework for math was to cover our textbook and do three of the sheets in our State Student Assessment Survey preparation packets. The tests were only three weeks away, and Mr. Pierce was all hopped up about them.

I picked up my packet from the stack on Mr. Pierce's desk on my way out of the room while Jake pretended not to notice they were there. "The ass tests," he said. "I can't wait. We don't have homework during the test week, and we spend the three hours a day of test time just sitting in a classroom doing nothing."

That pretty much describes every day of Jake's life.

I got out into the hallway and took off, trying to get away from Jake as fast as I could and on to my next class.

Which was art, one of those classes, like music, that everybody is supposed to really enjoy. Ah . . . why? At least my art class was going to be taught by Mr. Ruby, the cool art teacher, and not the old hippy woman who was always spitting sunflower seed shells into her hand.

When I got to the art room, the first thing I saw was Luke Slocum, my best friend from elementary school, putting his backpack down at an empty table. Luke! Empty table! I rushed over, afraid three other people would get there before me and take all the empty seats.

"Hey," I said to him as I sat down. Luke was the first person I'd seen that day who I actually wanted to say hello to. I hoped that "hey" was a much cooler way of doing it.

"Hey," Luke said back.

Someone came up behind me and dropped onto one of the empty stools at our table.

"Can you believe it? We're both in this class, too," Jake said.

I watched Luke turn and start looking around the room for another empty seat. We'd hardly seen each other for a whole year. I couldn't really expect him to stick by me through good times and bad, particularly if the bad times included Jake Rogers.

Luke slowly stood up, as if he wasn't sure what he should do. Three more kids came in and took seats while he tried to make up his mind. That left two tables with one empty chair each—a table of girls and ours. Luke picked up his backpack and started toward the girls' table, but another boy beat him there.

He came back, sighed, and sat down. He was pretty quiet the rest of the period. Or maybe he just seemed that way since Jake was making so much noise whispering hello to everyone.

My third-period class was social studies, which is probably my best subject. I was walking down the hall toward the classroom when I realized I was following a blond girl who was nearly as tall as I was. A girl who looked smart and cool even from the back. A girl lots of people were speaking to as she walked along. A girl who was turning into my classroom!

Chelsea Donahue was walking into my classroom! Right in front of me! I could reach out and touch her! Which I would never do, but that's how close I was to her.

Chelsea and I are going to be in the same social studies

44

class again this year, I thought as I followed her. I'm going to sit closer to her this time. I'm going to—

Chelsea got away from me because I was distracted by the sight of what I assumed was Ms. Cannon, our teacher—a pretty woman in a heavy sort of way. She was wearing a pair of red leather pants that looked as if they were at least a size and a half too small for her and balancing all her weight on tiny red high-heeled shoes with open toes and no backs.

By the time I was able to take my eyes off her, a lot more people were in the room. Most of them, I noticed, had been in my social studies class—and on the honor roll—the year before. I started to get a bad feeling.

I hurried up to the front of the room and said, "Hello, Ms. Cannon?"

I had done it again—said the "H" word. And what was worse, in my rush to speak to Ms. Cannon, I hadn't noticed that she was busy with—who else?—Melissa Esposito. I hated to interrupt, but I'd sort of already done it with the "hello." So since I had Ms. Cannon's attention, I went ahead and asked, "Ah, Ms. Cannon, could you tell me if this is accelerated social studies?"

She nodded her head, and I said in a low voice, "Would you check your list to see if I'm supposed to be here? My name's Kyle Rideau."

Ms. Cannon froze for a second before looking down at a computer printout.

"Your name's here," she said, and I groaned.

Her eyes narrowed. "Is that a problem?" she asked. "Because if it is, let's get it taken care of right now. Education is very important to me. I'm working on a Ph.D., and I expect all my students to be as committed to their studies as I am to mine. So if you think you're going to want out of here, let me write you a pass to the guidance office before we waste another minute of each other's time."

I promised myself I would get my hello problem under control and never use the word again. Then I looked over my shoulder at Chelsea. I decided I'd skip the trip to the guidance office.

"I'm fine," I said to Ms. Cannon. "I was just checking. Nice outfit you have on," I added as I backed away.

I slunk off to an empty desk. It just happened to be behind Bradley Ryder. Bradley is smart, but he's not weird about it the way Melissa and some of the other kids in accelerated classes are. He doesn't act as if he thinks he's on some kind of mission from God to make the world a better place or find a cure for cancer or something just because he's always read above grade level. That's why people don't hate him even though he's in all kinds of accelerated classes, plays first trumpet in the band and first base in baseball, got the best part in the Drama Club's play last year, and goes skiing over winter vacation with his family instead of sitting around waiting for his mom to get home with the car. He never even had to wear braces, and you just know he's never going to have acne.

He turned around to me and whispered, "Bet she assigns a lot of homework."

46

Brad is also always right. In addition to covering our social studies textbook, Ms. Cannon told us to read the first section of chapter one and prepare to discuss the review questions. We had to do three pages in our SSASie preparation packets for Thursday, and she warned us that on Friday we would be discussing current events, so we should start watching the news for something to talk about.

On my way to my next class, I thought about all the hours I'd put in on social studies projects back in sixth grade and wondered if seventh grade social studies could be that much worse. Of course it could. Things can always be worse.

With my mind occupied like that, it took me a while to notice that a lot of the kids from social studies were walking along with me to English. Just as I realized that I must have accelerated English with them again this year, I heard "Hellooo, Kyle!" being shouted at me from somewhere in the crowded hallway. I pretended I didn't hear it and followed Melissa and Chelsea into our next classroom.

But Jake had seen where I was going.

"Hellooo, Kyle," he repeated from the doorway. The words roared out of him as if he were using a microphone and speaker.

He didn't actually come into the room, though. He held on to the door casing with each hand and leaned into the room as if there were some kind of force field keeping him from entering honor roll airspace.

Did this mean that in an accelerated class I was safe from him?

"Hel-hello," I said, to make sure I didn't tick him off and because I really couldn't help myself.

"What are you doing in here with these snots?" he asked.

What could I say that would satisfy him but not get the accelerated kids on my case? They had to notice he was there talking to me.

Suddenly a man in a dark dress shirt and tie marched to the back of the classroom and closed the door in Jake's face, which took care of the problem for me. Jake pounded on the door from the outside a couple of times and finally gave up and moved on.

Mr. Borden, my new English teacher, turned around and looked at me. His hair was a little too long, and he had to toss his head so his bangs wouldn't hang in his eyes. "A friend of yours?" he asked.

"Ah . . ."

The room was totally quiet. All the other students were looking at me, as if they'd been wondering about that, too.

"He's more like a stalker," I explained.

A couple of boys behind me laughed.

Mr. Borden stared at me. Then all of a sudden he said, "Stalking is not funny," and marched back to his desk before I had a chance to say something like "Tell me about it!" or "Was I laughing?"

For homework we had to cover our English textbook and do three pages of vocabulary words. We also had to write an essay for Friday. The topic was "Are we alone?" Mr. Borden said he had gotten it off an old SSASie test and that it should give us practice writing the kinds of boring things the people who score those tests like.

My classmates disappeared at the end of the period, probably for another accelerated class. I was left to face my lunch section by myself.

Lunch on the first day of school is worse than gym because gym is supposed to be an ordeal but lunch isn't. You're supposed to enjoy it. But there are three lunch sections, and on the first day of school you have to walk into the cafeteria not knowing who has been assigned to yours. Will your friends be there? Will you be able to eat with them? Will you have to sit by yourself at the end of a table pretending to read a book or doing homework while everyone around you *knows* that you're really just putting on a show for them?

I got into line. Water freezes faster than that lunch line moved, which meant I had lots of time to worry about where I would actually eat. I pulled the first two things I could find that wouldn't damage my braces onto my tray, paid for them, and started looking for a table.

The cafeteria was crawling with desperate kids trying to find people to eat with. I passed the first row of tables. No one I knew. I passed the second row of tables. Full of new sixth-graders.

When I got to the third row, I noticed that there was a table way at the back of the room with only three people. One of them was Jake Rogers. He was sitting with a couple of eighth-graders—Brian Coxmore, who is sixteen years old and still in eighth grade, and Kenny Ferris, whose older brother is in jail. Kenny is expected to follow him there soon.

I had to find a table before I got back to them. I had to find a table before Jake saw me.

I moved closer and closer to the point where Jake's Kyle Radar would pick me up. Once he sucked me into eating lunch with him, my future would be crystal clear. No one would ever believe that I wasn't one of Jake Rogers's badass friends. My hands were sweating so badly, I could feel my Styrofoam tray dissolving from the moisture. My head swung from side to side as I scanned the cafeteria, looking for a friendly face near a free chair. Or even just a free chair.

I was thinking that it would be a perfect time for a fire drill when I saw Luke. And there, at the end of his table, was an empty chair. I held my breath while I slid between seats and kept my face turned away from Jake, just in case he tried to signal to me. I didn't ask if the free seat was taken, I didn't wait to be invited, I just dumped my tray on the table and collapsed onto the chair.

"You guys have got to let me sit here," I pleaded. "Otherwise I'm going to get stuck sitting with Jake and those guys he hangs out with. He's already in two of my classes, and he follows me in the hall. I can't get away from him."

"Oh, Kyle, man, having Jake like you is almost as bad as having him *not* like you," Luke said, sounding pretty sympathetic when you consider that he'd had to sit with Jake in art because of me.

"It's worse," I insisted. "At least if Jake pounds on you on your way to the buses after school, you might get some pity. Nobody pities Jake's friends."

"Most people are afraid of Jake's friends," a guy named Ted added.

I looked around the table. In addition to Luke and Ted, who I recognized from my two months in Boy Scouts, there was someone who'd been in a study hall with me last year, plus two guys I didn't know. None of them acted as if they were thrilled to see me, but they didn't seem to think I was going to grab a plastic knife off someone's tray and use it on them, either.

"Jake has already been sent to the office today. He's in my English class," Luke explained. "Mrs. Hooker was walking up the aisle, and Jake waits until she's right next to him and then he . . . and then he . . . farts! It sounded just like a dog howling! A wolf! Mrs. Hooker turns to him with this really mad look on her face, and she starts to say something, but Jake holds up his hands and says, 'It's okay, Mrs. Hooker. I'll take the blame for you. I don't mind.' So she sends him to the principal!"

I was laughing around my french fries, a safe item for me to eat because I can stick them way back and chew them where they won't make a disgusting mess all over the front of my braces.

"What do you think he said when Mr. Alldredge asked why Hooker sent him there?" Luke gasped, hardly able to talk, he was laughing so hard. "She farted?"

"Remember when we were kids and we took swimming lessons with Jake and he farted in the pool?" I asked.

"There's a memory that definitely makes me glad I decided not to take swimming lessons this year," Luke said.

Swimming lessons was another one of the things, like Boy Scouts, that I quit last year because of homework.

"I'm taking taekwondo with Ted instead," Luke announced, nodding at Ted, who was sitting across from me.

Those french fries I'd been eating suddenly felt as if they'd re-formed into a solid potato down under my ribs. Luke was taking taekwondo with Ted. Luke used to do things with me. Seeing that you've been replaced by someone else is the strangest feeling. It's like when people in movies find out they have a clone and realize that there's nothing special about them anymore because someone else can be them as well as they can.

"How can you start taking taekwondo in seventh grade?" I asked him, hoping I didn't sound upset. "You can't start any sport in seventh grade. It's too late. You have to already know how to play so you'll be good enough to make the middle school teams."

"Trotts doesn't have any martial arts teams. We started taking taekwondo at the taekwondo school in the next town this past July," Ted said. "It doesn't matter how old you are when you start. You can even start when you're an adult. The guy who runs the school gives new students a private lesson to show them kicks and stuff, and then you start training in classes with other people on your level. And guess what? Mr. Goldman says we're big enough and strong enough to train with adults."

"We thought taekwondo would be a cool thing to do while we're waiting for the next Master Lee movie to come out in November. Besides, Holly Cappa takes taekwondo," Luke confided—to everyone at the table. "If we're in class together, it will be like going out on a date."

Ted rolled his eyes. "Holly Cappa is a high green belt. She won't even practice with us because we're three ranks below her. She's always trying to hang around Chelsea and this high-school girl who are both red belts."

"Chelsea Donahue?" I squeaked casually.

"Yeah. She's been taking taekwondo for a while. She and Holly started when they were little and moved up to the adult classes when they were big enough. That's why they're so far ahead of us," Luke explained.

"How often do you have to go to class?" I asked.

"Two or three times a week," Ted said.

"Two or three times a week!" I repeated. "And you still go to Boy Scouts, too? How do you do all that and get your homework done?"

The bell rang and Luke got up to carry his tray to the trash can. "We don't have that much. Besides, there are taekwondo classes every night and on Saturday morning. You just go to the ones you can get to."

But I can't get to anything. And if I could get to things, who would I go with? Oh, yeah. That's right. *Nobody!*

53

The rest of us stood up. Right at that moment, someone grabbed my arm. I turned around and saw Jake.

He signaled to his two buddies. "We're off to the bathroom to have a smoke. You wanna come?"

It was the first invitation I'd had since before I started sixth grade.

"I have to go to my locker before my next class," I said.

"You wussing out?" Jake asked, looking as if he might be beginning to suspect that I was trying to avoid him.

"No. No," I assured him. "Maybe another time."

My fifth-period class was health and living, and Mrs. Haag from my advisory was my teacher. Health and living isn't included in State Student Assessment Surveys, so all we had to do for homework was have our parents sign a form stating that it was okay for us to watch sex education videos. This happens every year. My mother not only thinks it's okay for me to watch sex ed videos, she insists that I see them.

I'm not sure what happened during sixth period because none of it was in English. Everyone said *hola* to the teacher because she made us, so for the first time all day I wasn't the only one sounding like a reject. I had to guess that our homework was to cover our textbook because she gave us the assignment in Spanish.

You'd think I'd look forward to seventh period, it being the last one of the day. But seventh period was going to be science. Science is always disappointing because it's never like the stuff you see in science fiction shows.

When I got to science class, Beth and Jamie were already

there. They were all excited because they hadn't been together since lunch. They had spent the last two periods writing in notebooks they were trading so both girls could read all about what each of them had to say during the last hour and fifty-three minutes of their lives. Not much would be my guess.

Luke came in right after me, and we took seats across the aisle from each other. Okay, so maybe science wouldn't be so bad.

Then Jake arrived.

He came running over and threw himself into the seat behind me.

"Say it," he told me.

I knew immediately what he was talking about. How could I not know after what had been going on that day? But I didn't want to say it, and I didn't want to admit that I knew what he meant because that would be admitting that I'd been doing something unusual that day. Something that he, and maybe everyone else, had noticed. So I tried to act all casual, and I asked him, "Say what?"

"Hello."

"You want me to say hello to you?"

"Not to me," he said, as if I were some kind of moron. "To her."

I looked over at Jamie and Beth, who were now watching us as if they thought we might do something so awful they would have to jump up and run for their lives.

"Not them, either. Her."

He pointed to the teacher.

I felt this little rush of panic as I realized that I hadn't spoken to my new science teacher when I came into the room. Then I thought, Since when have you cared about that?

"It's too late. She's busy now. I'd just be bothering her," I said to Jake.

"Exactly." He laughed.

"I don't think teachers really like to have people say hello to them. You know, like Mr. Pierce this morning?" I reminded him.

"Yeah, that was great. Go ahead. Say hello to the old lady up there."

A couple of kids overheard that and snickered.

"Mr. Pierce didn't even know I was the person who said hello to him this morning. *You're* the one he heard when *you* said hello to him," I pointed out. "So, uh, why don't you do it?"

Jake looked toward the front of the room and started waving his hand. "Hey! You up there! Teacher! Kyle has something he wants to say."

All situations that involve Jake end up being at least strange, if not nasty and ugly. But the particularly strange part of that particular strange Jake situation was that if I had thought to say hello to the science teacher when I came into the room, none of what was happening just then would have happened. So in a strange, twisted way, I was to blame for my own problem.

"Well, what is it?" the teacher said.

"Nothing. Really. It's okay to start class," I answered, desperately trying to move everyone's attention away from me and on to something else.

Jake gave me a punch in the middle of the back that made me cry out. I had to remind myself that he was supposed to like me.

"Okay, okay," I snapped over my shoulder at him. Then I looked at the teacher and in the most normal voice I could manage said, "Hello, Mrs. Lynch."

"Don't be a smart-ass," she replied.

Usually I would have agreed with all the kids in the room who were laughing. There is something very funny about a teacher using the word "ass." But here's the thing—it's only funny when she's using the word about someone else.

Of course, she wasn't using it about Jake. So he laughed and laughed and laughed.

CHAPTER 5

☹ ☹ ☺ ☺ ☹ ☹

"Sweetheart, are you *sure* things were really that bad?" Mom asked after she got home from work and I told her what had happened on my first day of seventh grade.

"Ah, let me think . . . yes! Yes, they were that bad!" I exclaimed.

"Well, uh, you do have that little problem with looking for the worst in every situation. You know, negativity?" Mom said. "And then you get yourself all wound up about it."

"I didn't have to look," I told her. "People do *not* like to hear the word 'hello.' It leads to nothing but trouble. Since when do I go around saying hello to people, anyway? I don't know what happened to me. I must have been nervous or something."

"That's true," Lauren said. "I don't think I've ever heard anyone accuse you of being friendly."

All of a sudden Mom started to laugh. "I know what happened. It was the book. *Happy Kid!* Remember? You read that chapter about great relationships beginning with the word 'hello.' And then you used what you'd read in your daily life. That's wonderful. I'm proud of you."

"I didn't do that," I objected. "That book's stupid. I forgot what I read just as soon as I read it."

"You gave your grandmother a nice big hello on the phone when she called this morning," Mom reminded me.

"That was a joke," I said. But then I remembered saying hello to my father that morning when I didn't even have to because he was still asleep.

"It wasn't very funny when he was saying hello to everyone on the bus," Lauren pointed out. "More . . . weird, I'd say."

"Well, we are talking about someone who's terribly out of practice," Mom admitted. "You can't expect perfection with the first effort."

I stopped working on making covers for my textbooks for a moment and stared into space while I recalled passing on something I'd read in the newspaper to Jamie and Beth the way Mom's book had suggested. And I thought I remembered complimenting someone on her outfit, too. That had definitely come right out of *Happy Kid!* I'd never have thought of something like that on my own.

I turned to my mother. "This is all your fault! None of this would have happened if you hadn't made me read that stupid book. I had a plan, you know. I was going to be *really* quiet because nobody notices *really* quiet kids. Nobody accuses them of things. That was all I wanted this year—to be ignored. But you can't be really quiet *and* go around saying hello to everybody you see! You have to do one or the other!"

"I think it's a good thing the book ruined that plan of yours. Did you seriously think you'd enjoy being ignored for a whole year?" Mom asked.

"I'll never know now, will I?"

Mom sighed. "Give the book another chance," she insisted.

"You probably just did something wrong, anyway," Lauren said.

"How can somebody say hello wrong?" I asked her.

"You tell me. You're the one who did it."

Lauren and I were sitting at the kitchen table with her boyfriend, Jared, who was helping me with the book covers while my mother threw together some dinner. Lauren was sitting with her head on the kitchen table and her eyes closed. She gets pretty bored whenever she's not the subject of a conversation.

"You got to eat lunch with Luke," Mom pointed out. "Why can't you be happy about being in the same lunch section with him?"

"Happy about eating lunch with him so I can find out he's replaced me with Ted Fenton? I don't think so. They go to *taekwondo* together, by the way. Am I going to taekwondo? No, I'm not."

"You could go if you wanted to," Mom said eagerly. "It would be terrific for you to do something after school."

"I'm already doing something after school. It's called homework. I can't go to taekwondo because on top of everything else," I said, "I'm in accelerated English and social studies again this year."

"Uh-oh," Mom said. "Do you want me to call the guidance office and get you out of them?"

"No! Why would I want you to do that?"

"Because you wanted me to get you out of them last year," Mom replied.

"That's because they put me in those classes by mistake last year," I reminded her.

"And it's not a mistake this year?" Lauren asked.

"How did you get into accelerated classes by mistake?" Jared asked as he finished one of my books and reached for an old paper grocery bag so he could get started on another.

"I don't know," I said. "*I* didn't make the mistake."

Lauren very unhelpfully explained. "Kyle actually sat in the classes for three weeks before he realized they were for accelerated students. Doesn't that suggest he didn't belong there? Wasn't that proof that someone had done something terribly, terribly wrong?"

"Hey, there were a lot of kids in those classes from the other elementary schools in town," I objected. "How was I supposed to know they were smart?"

"Didn't you try to do something when you found out about the mistake?" Jared asked.

Lauren and I looked at our mother.

"What was I supposed to do?" Mom asked. "Go to the school and tell them my baby wasn't smart enough to be in with those kids?"

"You're a counselor, Mom. You couldn't have thought of a better way to put it?" I demanded. "Something not so . . . negative?"

"I tried."

"Yeah, well, not fast enough." I turned back to Jared. "While we were fighting about it, another week passed. I'd been in those two classes for a month. If I'd dropped them then, I would have been a month behind in the regular classes I picked up. Who knows how long it would have taken me to catch up?"

"The rest of your life?" Lauren suggested.

I ignored her and said to Jared, "So there I was, in these two 'special' classes, and the only way I could get out of them would be to join two classes that weren't special but that I was a month behind in, so I'd have to work extra hard to catch up. What was the point? Work hard in one class or work hard in the other."

"Wow, talk about irony," Jared said, nodding his head in appreciation.

None of Lauren's other boyfriends ever used words like "irony." Jared definitely is a step up for our family.

"Look what I figured out today," I said, pulling my class schedule out of my pocket. "See the list of classes? You notice how both English and social studies have the letter 'A' after them?"

"Oh, no," Mom sighed. "It must stand for 'accelerated.' I can't believe we didn't notice that. How embarrassing."

"Why?" Lauren asked. "You never gave it a thought because you never expected Kyle to be dumped in classes for A-kid types. He is a B-minus type, after all."

"It doesn't matter what type you are," I said as I folded up my schedule. "The people at Trotts stick you in a class somewhere and keep you there. You wait and see. They're going to put me in A-kid classes next year, too."

"Next year you'll be in eighth grade," Lauren pointed out, as if I couldn't work that out for myself. "Instead of accelerated classes, the eighth-grade A-kids at Trotts take ninth-grade classes. I had a great time in ninth grade. We—"

"You mean they skip a grade?" I broke in, because once Lauren gets started down Memory Lane, she's sometimes there a long time, reliving every sleepover and trip to the mall.

"Oh, no, no, no," Jared answered for Lauren. "They don't actually go to high school themselves. Teachers from the high school walk across the parking lot to teach classes in ninth-grade English, math, science, or social studies to what Lauren calls the A-kids. They take their gym, health and living, and electives with the rest of the eighth grade. But then they won't have to take ninth-grade English, say, with all the other ninth-graders when they're really in ninth grade. They'll take tenth-grade English instead."

"Why would anyone want to do that?" I asked. It seemed kind of complicated to me, and for what?

"They do it so that they'll finish taking required courses a year or two before they graduate. Then they'll have time to take more advanced-placement college-level classes than the other kids will have time for." Jared grinned. "I'm taking precalculus this year, myself."

"College-level classes!" I repeated. "I don't want to take college-level classes! I don't want to take precalculus!"

"Don't worry," Lauren assured me. "With the grades you get in math, you're never getting near a precalc course."

"Kyle, stop worrying. You don't have to think about taking college-level courses for years," Mom said. "And while math may not be your subject, your grades in your accelerated classes have been just fine. The problem is how hard you had to work to get them."

Mom was right. My last two years of high school were ages away. In the meantime, I'd decided I wanted to stay with the A-kids.

"It doesn't matter how hard I have to work," I told her. "I've got to stay in those accelerated classes now. I don't want people to think I *can't* stay in them."

I particularly didn't want Chelsea Donahue to think I couldn't stay in an A-kid class. Chelsea Donahue, who was smart and athletic and really good-looking. Someday, if we got a chance to talk, I hoped I could make her understand that it was just a big foul-up when she saw me walking with a state trooper in the school lobby back in June. And then we would hold hands and walk to all our classes together. My whole life would become better. Great, in fact. But it would never happen if I didn't stay in A-kid English and social studies.

Not that I could say anything about Chelsea to my mother

and sister. You really have to be careful about telling family members anything important. They're always going to be around, and you never know when they'll remind you of stuff you'd really rather not think about—like how back in seventh grade you liked Chelsea Donahue, who was too smart and too good-looking for you.

"Besides," I added, wanting to make sure they didn't suspect anything, "A-kid English and social studies are the only places I can be rid of Jake. No one is going to mistake *him* for an A-kid."

Once we finished with my textbook covers, I went back to my room to get a little more homework done before dinner. I'd already done the SSASie review sheets for math and social studies. I didn't have any for science. Mrs. Lynch wasn't giving us any review work because she said she wasn't going to risk having anyone accuse her of helping a student cheat. I'd only known her for less than an hour, but I didn't think she had to worry about anyone accusing her of helping a student do anything.

But that meant the only review work I had left was the most important. Not that I cared that much about getting ready for the yearly SSASies. I'd always done really well on them, and I didn't want to mess with success by going overboard studying. I could end up making things a whole lot worse doing something like that.

No, the review work I had left, the "Are We Alone?" essay for Mr. Borden, was important because Chelsea was in his class. I had spent all of sixth grade sitting in two classes with her. Maybe I could spend all of seventh grade making a good impression on her. Then, when we were together next year in those ninth-grade English and social studies classes, we could talk on the phone a few times. And then when we were together in whatever kind of A-kid courses they had at the high school, we could spend all our time between classes together. Then in eleventh grade . . . I'd have someone to go with me to the Junior Prom!

So I sat down at the crummy old computer I had inherited when my grandmother upgraded hers, which is all I have in my room because my parents insist it's just fine for doing homework. I opened a new file and typed "Are We Alone?" at the top of the screen. Then I typed "No."

I deleted the "No" and started again.

```
                Are We Alone?
    Some people ask, Are we alone? The answer
is no.
```

Well, there's one paragraph, I thought. Then I went on.

```
                Are We Alone?
    Some people ask, Are we alone? The answer
is no.
    Merriam-Webster's Collegiate Dictionary
defines "alone" as "separated from others,"
"isolated," "exclusive of anything or any-
one else."
```

Uh-oh, I thought as I closed the dictionary and dropped it on the floor. That means the answer is yes.

Are We Alone?
Some people ask, Are we alone? The answer is yes.

Merriam-Webster's Collegiate Dictionary defines alone as "separated from others," "isolated," "exclusive of anything or anyone else." Even if there are aliens in the universe, we are separate from them and isolated, and so we are alone.

I thought that sounded really intelligent and deep, as if I spent a lot of time thinking, which is exactly how A-kid papers sound.

Then I kind of drew a blank.

I sat at my desk and kicked at some stuff on my floor while I tried to think. I hit something that was hidden under my pajama bottoms. I kept kicking and thinking and kicking and thinking. After a while, I was kicking and not thinking and kicking and not thinking. I don't know how long I went on like that before I finally looked down and saw that what I had been kicking was the copy of *Happy Kid!* I'd thrown on the floor that morning after I'd finished with it.

Since work on my essay had come to a halt, I thought I'd put my time to good use by reading another chapter. I didn't have to do anything the book told me to, after all. I could just read a chapter and get a dollar. So I opened up *Happy Kid!* and once again started to read the first thing I found.

Does Your Life Stink or Is It YOU?

Say you wake up to a beautiful day and spend it being miserable because you have to go to school. Or you get a B-minus on a paper and wish it were an A. Or you have an opportunity to eat lunch with a friend and all you can think about is how bummed out you are because the friend is spending time with someone else later. You could be one of those people who only see the worst in every situation. Think about it. Does your life actually stink, or do you just think it does?

I had to laugh when I read that. Just how is a person supposed to be able to tell if his life stinks or he just thinks it does? And couldn't you turn that question around? "Is your life really great or do you just think it is?" I thought I'd like to hear a happy person answer that.

What I should have been feeling was surprise that I just *happened* to stumble upon this passage that just *happened* to be about the exact thing my mother just *happened* to have been nagging me about for days. But she had bought me the book, after all, so I never gave it a thought.

CHAPTER 6

☹ ☺ ☺ ☺ ☹ ☺

You can never find a bookmark when you want one, at least not in my room, so I left *Happy Kid!* open facedown on the floor for a couple of days to mark my place. I must have broken the rigid binding when I left it on the floor, because the next few times I tried to read a new chapter and make a dollar, it opened up to the same place. "Does Your Life Stink or Is It YOU?" The rest of the book was as stiff as it had ever been, though, because when I tried to intentionally open it to a new page, I couldn't keep it open long enough to finish reading what was there. As soon as I moved my hands from the sides of the book so I could read what was under them, the pages started flipping and the first thing I knew, there I was again at "Does Your Life Stink or Is It YOU?"

I started becoming very self-conscious about using deodorant.

I was finally able to open the book to a new chapter the next Monday morning. Unfortunately, the new chapter was a lot like the one I'd been reading over and over again. I just had time to complain to my mother and collect a dollar from her before I had to leave the house.

I had to go to the orthodontist. With my *grandmother.* She owns a real estate agency and can take time off much more easily than either of my parents. That's why I end up spending way too much time with her.

"This morning I'm missing math so I can go to the orthodontist. Is that a good thing because I hate math, or is it a bad thing because I'm terrible at it, so I really ought to be in class learning all I can?"

"You lost me," Nana replied.

I pulled *Happy Kid!* out of my backpack and it fell open in my hand.

"Would you look at this?" I said. "Last week this book kept opening up to the same spot because I wrecked its binding. This morning I finally got it to open to something new, and now it just opened up to that same place again. There must be something wrong with this thing."

"I'm still lost," Nana said.

"I can explain everything. I brought this book with me to read in the doctor's office because Mom said she'd give me a dollar for every chapter I finish. The chapters are really short, by the way, so it's not a big deal. Here's the chapter I read this morning while I was waiting for you to pick me up."

Make Sure You're Getting the *Real* Picture!

The first step in solving that negativity problem is recognizing it exists. Make a list of all the times you look for the worst in life and find it. Are the items on your list really the *worst*? Or do you just think they are because that's what you were looking for?

"You're not trying to suggest that I have a negativity problem, are you?" Nana asked. "I get enough of that kind of thing from your mother, thank you very much."

"I get that from her, too! She says I look for the worst in every situation. That's why she got me this book. She thinks it will make me happy."

Nana and I both laughed.

"The last chapter I read says that if you're one of those people who *does* see the worst in every situation, then your life really isn't all that bad, you just think it is. So it would actually be a *good* thing if we're negative. Can you believe it? That would mean that our lives are good, we just don't know it."

"Really?" Nana said. "Be sure to explain that to your mom."

"The thing is, I couldn't figure out how to tell if something's actually bad or if I just think it is. Then this morning I opened this book up and found this chapter I just read you that explains how to do it. Make a list."

"So this is what you've been spending your time thinking about, huh?" Nana asked as she turned into Dr. Allegretti's parking lot.

"This and how I can get my homework done faster so I can take taekwondo," I said.

"Taekwondo?" she repeated as she parked the car. "Good for you, Kyle! In this day and age, we all have to be prepared to defend our way of life."

Defend our way of life? I thought. Wasn't she talking about fighting terrorists? I just wanted to get to know a girl.

Once we were in Dr. Allegretti's office, I let my grandmother have the only seat left. It was on the couch between the bald man with the purple splotch on his head and the woman who kept apologizing because the baby she was holding smelled. I sat on the floor, pulled a piece of paper out of my backpack, and wrote "Things I *Think* Are Bad That Are *Really* Good."

When I left the office forty minutes later, the wire that went through the brackets on my lower teeth had been pulled so tight that tears had come to my eyes. And there was nothing on my list.

I didn't realize I'd left my backpack in Nana's car until I got to the school office so I could get my late pass. The thing weighs nearly thirty pounds. How could I not have noticed I wasn't carrying it? Of course, my mother's note explaining why I was late was in the backpack.

I was trying to tell the secretary what had happened when someone behind her shouted, "Yo! Kyle!"

I looked over the secretary's shoulder and there was Jake standing next to the principal, Mr. Alldredge.

"Gus, can't we do something to help out my man Kyle?" Jake said to Mr. Alldredge.

Gus? I thought as Mr. Alldredge snapped "In there" at Jake and pointed toward the door to his office.

"Hey, I tried," Jake called to me as he went in.

Mr. Alldredge stepped over to the attendance window.

"You're Jake Rogers's man now, are you?" he asked. Though it wasn't really a question. It was more of an accusation.

"He—not—I—no," I stammered.

Mr. Alldredge shook his head in disgust, and the secretary handed me an unexcused late pass, meaning that if I didn't bring a note the next day, my first two period teachers didn't have to let me make up whatever work I'd missed.

That didn't make the list.

I got into social studies halfway through the class, which meant that everybody looked at me as I walked through the door. I waved my bright red unexcused late pass in Ms. Cannon's direction.

"My homework is in my backpack and my backpack is in my grandmother's car, and my mouth hurts because I went to the orthodontist," I said as I slowly slid into my seat.

I hoped Chelsea noticed how much I was suffering.

"Do you know what would happen if I used that excuse at the university where I'm working on my Ph.D.?" Ms. Cannon asked me.

During the first week of school Ms. Cannon had managed to mention her Ph.D. nearly every day.

"You don't have braces, Ms. Cannon. No one would believe you had been to the orthodontist," I pointed out.

"You missed my point, Kyle. You have to pay attention to what you're doing. Tomorrow we'll have been in school just one week, and already you're leaving your things all over the place. For that matter, did you really have to schedule a doctor's appointment during school hours?"

By the time I got out of social studies class, I still had nothing on my list. Everything I thought was bad really was. If I'd been keeping a list called "Proof That Life Sucks," it would have been filling right up.

I was late getting out of class, so I was stuck walking to English by myself.

Anytime you're with someone at school, particularly someone you actually like or can at least get along with, it's an accident. Even in the hallways you might not see your friends if their schedules are a lot different than yours. So the halls at school are filled with people by themselves or pretending they're not by themselves, or, if they really are with other people, being loud about it like Jamie and Beth so that everyone will know they're not alone.

Why didn't I think of this being-by-yourself stuff last week while I was writing my "Are We Alone?" essay? I wondered. Talk about something that sounded intelligent and deep.

I saw Chelsea's head above the crowd up ahead of me. I would have liked to have gotten a little closer to her, maybe almost walked together, but I couldn't get past Jamie and Beth, who were squealing with Melissa about a note one of them had written.

I got to English and waited for Mr. Borden to ask us to

turn in our homework, when the whole sad story of my back-pack, my grandmother, and my trip to the orthodontist would have to be told again. But he didn't. Instead, he handed back the essays we'd turned in on Friday and announced that we were going to share them.

Was having to "share" my essay a good thing that I wasn't recognizing because I had a problem with negative thinking? No way.

"We're going to tear your essays apart in class so you can identify your writing weaknesses," Mr. Borden explained. "In the weeks to come we'll study classic essayists so you can see how writing should be done. I will not teach you to write. The masters will."

This speech got a lot of the A-kids all fired up. A lot of them love doing whatever the teachers want to do. I don't mean they're suck-ups like Melissa. I mean they've been brainwashed or something. They *always* want to do what the teacher wants to do and to think what the teacher thinks. I don't understand it. For instance, I *tried* to tell myself that it was really good that I was going to be studying classic essayists and learning something from the masters, whoever they were. But I couldn't help thinking that the word "classic" is almost always bad news unless you're talking about old movies. I bet the A-kids never gave that a thought.

Melissa read first because, basically, she's a show-off and loves the sound of her own voice. She read something very fancy about how much it hurt to stand under the stars at night and to see so many of them while there is only one of her. Personally, I think it's a very good thing that there's only one of her.

One of the other kids in the class said that Melissa hadn't written an essay, she'd written a poem. I had totally missed that because, though Melissa is always writing things she says are poetry, they never rhyme, so I have to take her word for it. Teachers, though, love poetry that doesn't rhyme. They can't get enough of the stuff. Sure enough, Mr. Borden said what Melissa had written was an okay poem. She grinned all over, anyway, and wriggled around in her seat from all the attention. I didn't gag, even though I wanted to.

"But that poem would get you very little credit with the people who score the SSASies," Mr. Borden went on.

The room went totally still. Melissa looked as if she'd been turned to stone.

"You know why? Because they're all hired hacks making minimum wage. You think scholars, trained critics, read these essays? Hell, no! They're all old ladies trying to supplement their Social Security checks or kids out of college who can't get jobs. They won't recognize a quality piece of writing like this. They're looking for something short and easy to understand—something a machine could score in seconds, the way a machine, in just seconds, scores the bubble-test portion of the SSASies."

Aha! I thought. That explains why I always do well on the SSASies. My writing samples are always as short as I can make them. And since I never use metaphors and not even many adjectives, what's not to understand?

The next reader began her essay with "As I walk through the hallways at school, I am surrounded by hundreds of people, and yet I am alone. No one is like me."

I couldn't believe it! I was listening to my essay! The essay I would have written if I'd thought of it while I was doing my homework instead of in the hall on my way to class.

Except it was written by . . . Chelsea.

She went on about the hallway being a world and the people in it being different countries. She said it was as if each person was a separate culture with a separate language that no one else spoke. Then she got into all this stuff about words being like ambassadors and how communication could bring all the countries in the hallway together just as it could bring all the countries in the real world together.

I definitely would never have said any of that because I wouldn't have thought of it in a hundred years. But we did both think about hallways.

Mr. Borden and the other kids in the class said her imagery was "unique," she had used an "extended metaphor," and she understood the essay format.

"That was really good," I said after everyone else was through talking. I thought contributing to the class discussion would make a good impression on Chelsea, especially since my contribution was all about her. My reward was to have Mr. Borden tell me that I should read next.

Are We Alone?

Some people ask, Are we alone? The answer is yes.

Merriam-Webster's Collegiate Dictionary defines alone as "separated from others," "isolated," "exclusive of anything or anyone else." Even if there are aliens in the universe, we are separate from them and isolated and so we are alone.

Say there is life on another planet. Say there is life on lots of other planets. What does it have to do with us? Do we see any of these other beings? Do we communicate with them? Do we exchange goods and services?

Scientists who spend millions of dollars searching the skies for signs of life believe that just finding some tiny signal that there are other intelligent beings would provide the human race with companionship. But would it? How would knowing that there are others on other planets who we can't talk with, see, or hear make us feel that we have companions in this universe? It would be just like posting a message at an on-line forum. You know there are other people there because you see their messages. But they never respond to yours. So just knowing that there are others there doesn't make you feel good. You just feel

worse than ever because you can't communicate with them.

Are we alone? Definitely.

If I had known I was going to have to read the essay
aloud, particularly in front of Chelsea, I would never have included the part about people in forums not writing back to
me. Not that that ever actually happened. Well, just once.

The rest of the class didn't mention the forums, though.
They were too busy talking about my poor topic sentences
and lack of transitions between paragraphs. They said that
even though I restated my thesis in my conclusion, as I was
supposed to, it still stunk. One kid thought I sounded depressed and should go see somebody.

"He quoted an authority," Bradley finally said when it became clear no one else had anything good to say. "That
always improves an essay."

"But not when the authority is a *dictionary*," Melissa objected. "That is so dull and trite."

I kept waiting for Chelsea to say something nice, since I'd
said something nice when she read what she'd written, but
my essay was so bad, she probably couldn't think of anything. My plan to spend all of seventh grade making a good
impression on her was off to a really slow start.

Lunchtime came and my list was still just a blank piece
of paper.

My lunch money was in my pants pocket, not my back-pack, so if I hadn't been in pain, I could have bought something to eat. Instead, I just sat moaning at our table in the cafeteria while Luke talked about Holly, who he'd seen in the lobby when he went to the movies Friday night with Ted and some other kids from his social studies class. I had spent Friday night at home playing a computer game on-line.

Then Luke started to practice counting to ten in Korean with Ted, who was taking some kind of test with him in tae-kwondo at the end of the month. I was thinking, Is it my imagination, or is being left out of absolutely everything a bad thing? So I didn't notice Mr. Kowsz limping across the cafeteria toward us carrying something until he was almost on top of us.

"I happened to be walking through the lobby on my lunch break and met your grandmother, Rideau. She brought this in for you," he said to me, handing me my backpack. He sort of jerked his head toward the cafeteria door. I looked and saw Nana standing there. She started waving at me. She'd gone home and changed into one of her real estate agent suits, high heels, makeup, and jewelry. She'd done her hair.

Mr. Kowsz leaned toward me a little bit, as if that were enough to make what he then said to me confidential, which it wasn't. "Your grandmother looks very familiar to me. I'm wondering if I know your grandfather. Is he still working?"

"He's dead," I told him.

I'm absolutely certain that for just a second that old coot smiled. Then he tried to look sad and told me he was sorry to hear that. If I had been him, I would have left after that. But he hung around, cleared his throat, got kind of nervous, and said, "Has he been dead long?"

That was a question I'd never expected to hear from him. "I don't know," I said. "He died before I was born."

"Really?" Mr. Kowsz replied. He looked over at my grandmother and gave her a smile and a little wave.

My mouth dropped open, which made the wires and brackets that had been tightened that morning rub against the inside of my mouth so suddenly that my eyes started watering again.

"She's not really that good-looking," I wanted to shout after Mr. Kowsz as he sort of hopped back across the cafeteria toward Nana. "She dyes her hair." But all I could get out was a little squeal, the way you do when you're trying to scream in a dream.

"Oh, Kyle, man," Luke said as we watched the two of them leave the cafeteria together. "Mr. Kowsz is going to hit on your grammy."

"Moo Kowsz is going to be your new grampy," one of the other guys added.

"Are the items on your list really the *worst*?" the author of *Happy Kid!* had asked. "Or do you just think they are?" I'd have to say that as far as Mr. Kowsz becoming my new grampy was concerned, we were definitely talking about the worst. The absolute worst.

81

CHAPTER 7

When my mother got home from work that afternoon, I told her she owed me another dollar. I showed her the chapter in *Happy Kid!* about recognizing negative thinking and explained that I'd kept a list of every negative thought I'd had all day just the way the book said I should.

"Oh, Kyle, that's wonderful! It's the most positive thing you've done in over a year, maybe more."

"There isn't anything on the list, Mom, because I'm not negative. Everything that happened today *was* bad."

Mom pounded the kitchen counter with her fist. You would have thought she'd just found out I'd been selling stolen goods or something.

"Do you think I want everything that happens to me to be so awful?" I asked her. "I would love to find out that I'm negative and that things really aren't all that bad. But how are leaving my backpack in Nana's car and having Ms. Cannon chew me out for being irresponsible and not having my homework anything but bad? Oh, and by the way, she thinks you shouldn't be making orthodontist appointments for me during the school day."

"What?"

"She told me that in front of the whole class," I said. "Wait. There's more. We had to read our essays out loud in English class, and everybody hated mine. Then I found out at lunch that Luke went to the movies last weekend with a bunch of kids from his social studies class I don't even know. Gym classes start this week, and today was my day to have gym instead of health and living. I was the only boy in the locker room wearing briefs instead of boxers. It's as if some announcement went out over the summer telling everybody to make the switch, and I didn't get it. I looked like a freak. I don't know what went on in Spanish because I don't *understand* Spanish. And then in science—"

"Honey, calm down. You know and I know that things just weren't that bad. You were able to eat lunch with Luke— that's a good thing. And underwear is nothing to get all excited about. I will buy you some boxers before your next class. As far as Spanish goes, would you like us to get you a tutor?"

"No! No, no, no!"

"Kyle, get a grip on yourself. You're just blowing everything all out of proportion."

"Oh, yeah?" I exclaimed. "Here's something I'm not blowing out of proportion. Moo Kowsz is after Nana. And I'm not the only person who thinks so. The guys at lunch said the same thing."

For a few seconds Mom stopped jabbering about how I couldn't tell what was going on in my own life. I think maybe she was stunned. Then she asked, " 'After Nana,' as in he wants to ask her out?"

"What other kind of 'after Nana' is there?"

Mom made me tell her every word Mr. Kowsz had said and how he looked and how Nana looked.

"This is wonderful!" she exclaimed.

"How can you possibly get that out of what I just said?"

"Do you know how many years it's been since your grandmother has had a date?" Mom asked me. Then she started jumping up and down and shouting for Lauren so she could tell her the whole thing.

"Get a grip, Mom," I told her. "You're blowing this all out of proportion."

Dad stayed calm when he heard about Nana and Mr. Kowsz. Too calm.

"Trotts is the gateway to hell," I reminded him, "and Mr. Kowsz is the gatekeeper! You have to do something to stop them from seeing each other. How much more embarrassment can I take?"

Dad laid his hands on my shoulders and smiled sadly. "Don't worry. You're going to find that there is no limit to the amount of embarrassment you can take. And by the time you get to be my age, you'll be so used to being embarrassed, you won't even notice anymore."

"That's something to look forward to," I said. "But what am I supposed to do in the meantime?"

"Try to remember that there are no documented cases of people dying of embarrassment. You can live a long and healthy life while being totally humiliated."

After dinner I went upstairs to do homework. I hadn't been able to get much done after school because I was so sure that the telephone was going to ring any minute and Nana was going to announce that Mr. Kowsz had asked her to go to bingo with him or something. I still had plenty of stuff to do that I hadn't even pulled out of my backpack yet. I worked for almost an hour, then reached into my backpack for my social studies book. Instead *Happy Kid!* came out.

I looked at it and thought how funny it was that Mom had bought it for me, because she really needed a self-help book herself. I ought to find her a book called *Get Real!* It could be filled with passages like "You're happy to have your mother-in-law go out with a guy who patrols middle-school bathrooms for evildoers as if he's some kind of undercover agent? Get real!" "You think it's just fine to be wearing the wrong kind of underwear in front of absolutely everybody? Get real!" Yeah, Mom needed a book that would wreck something for her the way *Happy Kid!* had wrecked the first day of school for me.

The stupid thing was just sitting there in my hand. What does a person do when he's holding a book? He either puts it down or opens it up. I'd been doing homework for an hour, and almost anything will distract a person at that point. So I opened the book up and read a page.

Something to Look Forward To

Okay, sometimes things really don't go the way you want them to. That's no reason to go nuts and get down on the whole world. Sometimes you have to wait for what you want. In fact, most times you have to wait for what you want. Just think of it as something to look forward to.

"Ahh!" I shouted and slammed the book shut. *Something to look forward to.* I had just said those very words to my father.

I figured I must have read the passage wrong, so I picked up *Happy Kid!* again, planning to try to find that same page and check it out. I didn't actually have to look at all. The book fell open wherever it would, and I looked down.

Something to Look Forward To

Okay, sometimes things really don't go the way you want them to. That's no reason to go nuts . . .

There it was, the same page.

I had spent enough time watching the Sci Fi Channel to be able to tell what was going on. The book's binding wasn't too tight. Not after all this time. No, the book was sending me *messages*. Wasn't it? Or was that just too crazy to be true? Maybe not. Because if there was a creepy book with super-powers anywhere in the area, wasn't *I* the most likely person to get stuck with it?

"Something to look forward to"? How could that be a message for me? What could I possibly have to look forward to?

Maybe . . . Chelsea? Talking on the phone with Chelsea? Walking in the halls with Chelsea? Going to the prom with Chelsea? Okay. That would be cool.

Over the next couple of days the book fell open to the exact same "Something to Look Forward To" spot whenever I held it by its spine and let it flop open on its own. It wouldn't go away. But if that chapter was a message for me, what was it supposed to mean?

I couldn't get it out of my mind. After a while, I started noticing things happening that I thought *might* relate to the passage in the book.

On Thursday afternoon, while Lauren was setting the table for dinner, she asked my mother—again—to buy her a car.

"No," Mom said without looking up from where she was chopping a lot of green peppers and onions, even though she knows I hate them.

"Okay, then. Can I take yours to the movies tomorrow night?"

"Why don't you take your brother with you?" Mom suggested.

"What?" Lauren and I both shouted.

"Tomorrow is Friday. Maybe Kyle would like to go to the movies, too."

I should never have told my mother about Luke going to

the movies without me. I should never tell my mother anything. I wanted to go to the movies with Luke. With Bradley. With a group of guys. With Chelsea! But with my sister?

"You only allow me to drive with one other teenager in the car," Lauren said. "I want that one other teenager to be Jared."

"Shouldn't your boyfriend be driving *you* to the movies instead of you driving *him*?" I asked.

"Oh, I don't want her riding with Jared," my mother objected.

"None of my friends have to follow these insane rules about having to have their driver's license for three months before they can have other teenagers in the car with them and another three months before they can have more than one," Lauren complained. "*And* my friends all have cars. What are we, Amish or something?"

"Lauren, dear, don't make fun of people who don't have your access to electricity, cosmetics, and zippers," Mom said.

Car fights can go on for hours at our house. Days even. I started to head back up to my room, when all of a sudden I realized something. "A car is something you need to wait for, Lauren. Think of it as something to look forward to," I said.

"I'm seventeen years old. I've looked forward to it long enough," she yelled at me.

"I was just pointing out that you shouldn't go nuts and get down on the whole world because you can't get what you want right away. And now that I've said that, I'll be on my way."

"Oh, wait, Kyle," Mom called when I had almost made it

out to the hallway. "*Do* you want a ride to the movies Friday night?"

"He can't sit with us," Lauren said. "Not that he'd want to because we're not going to see anything about depressed superheroes or geeks saving the world."

"That's supposed to be some kind of slam about *Master Lee II: The Undead*, isn't it? Well, it's not coming out until November," I told her. "And, no, I do not want to go to the movies Friday night. I plan to finish the book I'm reading for social studies then. It's an excellent book."

"Oh, honey, you can read another time. Are you sure you wouldn't enjoy getting out of the house?" Mom insisted.

"No, he wouldn't. He loves it here," Lauren said.

"She was talking to me!"

"Kyle, you've got to get out of this house," Mom said. "It's not healthy for you to be here all the time by yourself."

"If I had a car, I could take him places," Lauren offered. "Except not to the movies."

"I don't *mind* being here," I said. Though I did. The place was driving me crazy.

"Well, *I* mind," Mom said. She shouted it, actually. "I cannot stand seeing you here alone any longer! I don't want to hear that you have too much homework. You think of something you want to do, or I'll think of something for you."

Lauren looked from Mom to me and said, "Like what?"

"I've been thinking that maybe Kyle would like to do something at the new Teen Center," Mom suggested.

"Oh, Mom, nobody goes there," Lauren objected. "Please.

I can't have it get around that my brother has been going to the Teen Center."

Mom smiled at me. "There's always the youth group at the church here in town. I've met the woman who runs it many times, and I know she'd love to have you join them."

Both Lauren and I screamed, "No!"

"Taekwondo!" I shouted. "I'll do taekwondo!"

"Get me a car, and I'll drive him there," Lauren offered.

"What is going on in here?" Dad asked as he came in the back door. "I can hear you guys shouting out in the yard." He dropped his briefcase on the kitchen counter and sighed. "You know, I used to come in here after a hard day of work, and these sweet little creatures would come running up to me shouting 'Dada!' and throw their arms around me. Where did they go?"

"Dada!" Lauren shouted as she threw her arms around him. "Kyle is doing taekwondo, and I'm getting a car."

She had that only half right. I was going to do taekwondo, but owning a car was still something Lauren was going to have to look forward to.

After the way my mother had carried on about me doing something after school, I thought she'd shove me into the car and have me in a taekwondo class that very night. But no. Three more days passed, another school week had started, and I still wasn't enrolled at Goldman's Taekwondo with Luke and Ted.

And Chelsea.

"Your mother talked with my mother about it for forty minutes on Saturday," Luke said on Monday. "What's left to know?"

We were in art class, which was sort of like a study hall with pictures. Each day Mr. Ruby gave us a little lesson on some kind of cartooning, which seemed to be the only kind of art he did, and then carried his own sketchbook over to the window and left us to do pretty much whatever we wanted so long as we pretended to be drawing and didn't make enough noise to attract teachers from other rooms.

"My mother spent an hour and a half this weekend on-line doing research on how to choose a martial arts school," I told Luke. "I kept telling her she was wasting her time because I was going with you or I wasn't going at all, but nothing would get her out from in front of that monitor. She's planning to stop at a store after work today so she can buy a book on the subject. Then she'll have to read it. And *then* she says we have to make an appointment with Mr. Goldman so the two of us can meet him and discuss his educational philosophy."

"All my mother discussed with him was his fee," Luke said. "You know, once you finally sign up for classes, you'll still have to meet with Mr. Goldman for a couple of private lessons. He's got to show you how to do the kicks and tie the belt on around your dobok and give you a talk about self-control, being humble, and what he'll do to you if you hurt anybody."

"Oh. Well, that's something to look forward to. I hope."

That was when it hit me. It was so obvious. The message in *Happy Kid!* wasn't about Lauren having to wait for a car at all. It *was* about Chelsea. It was about me waiting to be with Chelsea—at taekwondo. It was about taekwondo being something I could look forward to.

I was practically jumping up and down on my stool, thinking, Yes! That is something I can look forward to! when I caught a glimpse of Mr. Kowsz looking in at us through the classroom's open door. I accidentally made eye contact with him, and he smiled at me. I gasped, my hand slid across my paper, and the superhero I'd been drawing was left looking as if he'd thrown himself on a long spear.

"Luke! Mr. Kowsz just smiled at me," I whispered.

"Uh-oh. His head looks just like a skull when he does that."

"I'll get rid of ol' Moo Kowsz for you," Jake offered without even looking up from the cartoon he was drawing of a guy putting out a fire without a hose . . . or a watering can, either. His right arm flew up in the air, and he gave Mr. Kowsz the finger. Mr. Kowsz whipped out his detention pad.

"That was so worth it," Jake said after Mr. Kowsz waved the detention at him and moved off to bother somebody else. "Moo is always hanging around people like you and me. He thinks we're troublemakers." Then he laughed and nudged me with his elbow. "We are."

"Mr. Kowsz is the one person in this school who really ought to know that I'm *not* a troublemaker," I insisted.

"Isn't Moo hot for your grandma?" Jake asked. "You think he's copped a feel yet?"

I squealed like Jamie and Beth, I'm embarrassed to say, and then I had to apologize to Mr. Ruby for interrupting his work.

"How do you know about that?" I hissed at Jake. "Not about copping a feel. I mean how do you know . . . anything . . . about Moo . . . Mr. Kowsz and my grandmother."

"I was in the cafeteria when he came in and asked you about her. She was standing there in the doorway drooling over him. I'm pretty sure I saw him put his hand on her ass as they were leaving," Jake said right out loud.

I cringed and closed my eyes, trying to shut that image out of my mind.

"My grandmother hasn't said anything about him, and no one in my family has the guts to ask her," I explained.

"You know her telephone number? They'll let me use the phone down in guidance. I'll find out what's going on for you," Jake offered.

"No, thanks," I said.

Finding out what was going on with Mr. Kowsz and my grandmother was definitely not something I was looking forward to.

Lauren was looking forward to hearing all the details of anything that happened between Mr. Kowsz and our grandmother, though. And when the third week of school passed with no Nana boyfriend news, Lauren took matters into her own hands.

Late on Sunday afternoon Nana, Lauren, and I were sitting out on my family's deck. Nana had come over to read our newspaper and drink our coffee the way she does every Sunday after she closes the office. Lauren was painting her toenails. I was finishing the next chapter in my vocabulary book. I didn't have any real homework because SSASie testing started the next day. I was spending the weekend trying to get ahead on my schoolwork so I'd have some free time after school. My mother had finally finished her background check on Mr. Goldman and scheduled my private taekwondo lessons. I would start actual classes in October.

Everything was very quiet and restful. Or as quiet and restful as it can be when you're trying to finish three pages of fill-in-the-blank vocabulary statements.

And then, all of a sudden, Lauren said, "How's your love life, Nana? Everyone wants to know, so I thought I'd ask before I leave to go over to Jared's for dinner."

"I don't have one," Nana answered.

"No tall, skinny guy has called to ask you to go to the casino or on one of those senior citizen bus trips?" Lauren asked while she put the finishing touches on her pedicure.

I wondered if I had time to get up and run away from home before this conversation went any further.

"I did have a nice man ask me to stop by the middle school any Wednesday or Thursday afternoon so he could show me the lamp bases he makes out of metal and wood," Nana admitted.

I shouted, "No!" and Lauren said, "Oh, what a lame way to get a woman's attention."

"He couldn't just ask me out for real," Nana explained as she flipped the pages of the newspaper. "We'd only met in the school lobby. It's not safe to go out with a man you've met like that. He could be anybody. That's how serial killers meet their victims, you know."

Lauren tried to say, "In school lobbies?" but I drowned her out by asking, "You know who he is, don't you?" Maybe I yelled it.

Nana nodded. "He introduced himself. I remembered his name because I remember everything that goes on in your life, Kyle. But, in case I didn't, he explained how he knew you. He was quite a gentleman."

"A gentleman?" I repeated. "Jake Rogers says he saw Moo put his hand on your backside. Gentlemen don't do that. Do they?"

She laughed. "He did not put his hand on my backside. Or anywhere else. But somebody said he did, huh? Oh, stop looking like that. I'm not going to go to see your 'Moo's' lamp bases. I work on Wednesday and Thursday afternoons."

Nana was not going to be seeing Mr. Kowsz again. Maybe finding out about that was what *Happy Kid!* had meant by "something to look forward to." It was definitely what I had wanted to happen, and I had had to wait for it, too. Everything fit into the *Happy Kid!* message.

What a relief.

I looked over at Nana, who was reading an article about security delays at airports. That was how I always thought of her—bending over a paper or watching a television reporter while she took in bad news. I had never noticed before that she was also always alone.

CHAPTER 8

☹ ☺ ☺ ☺ ☹ ☺

"How come we, like, have to take these tests?" Beth asked the next morning.

We were still in our advisory classroom because our advisory teachers give us the SSASies. Mrs. Haag was standing in front of us, her arms filled with our English test booklets and scoring sheets.

"All the schools in the state are being tested to make sure they're providing you with a high-quality education," she explained.

"Wait," Melissa said. "The schools are being tested, but we're taking the tests?"

Mrs. Haag laughed. "Funny, isn't it?"

Melissa and I were the only ones who laughed. I actually thought Mrs. Haag had said something funny, but Melissa was probably just sucking up.

"Oh, come on. Perk up, everybody," Mrs. Haag said to the rest of the class. "Listen, those of you who have health and living with me this afternoon will be getting a real treat. We're going to watch videos. I thought that would be a nice, relaxing way to spend some time after taking a big test."

Beth and Jamie started squealing and making their "ick" faces, and even Melissa had a hard time acting all excited about something a teacher had planned for her. We'd all seen the kinds of sex education videos health and living teachers like to show in class. They have this really strange way of being both embarrassing and boring at the same time.

Most of that morning's English test involved vocabulary. The hardest part about that was making sure you filled out the bubbles on the answer sheet correctly.

When we ran out of time for vocab, Mrs. Haag gave us permission to go on to the writing portion of the test. We had to write an essay on one of the two topics printed in the booklet. The first one was "What do you think someone your age can do to help achieve world peace?" I didn't think I could even squeeze out a couple of sentences on that subject. But the second topic was "Are we alone?"

I thought I could do a little better on that one.

I glanced over at Melissa just in time to see her turn toward me with this puzzled expression on her face. We looked away fast because the two of us just don't want to see that much of each other, plus we had to get writing. I didn't know what Melissa was thinking, but I couldn't believe my luck. How often do you sit down to take a big test and find an essay topic you've already had a chance to practice on the page in front of you?

My pencil stopped moving. Could this be what *Happy*

Kid! meant by something to look forward to? Was my life so pitiful that a good essay topic was what I'd been waiting for? I would have liked to have gone nuts and got down on the whole world about that, but I really didn't have time just then.

The essay was the last thing we had to do for testing that day. After Mr. Alldredge announced over the intercom that we were out of time, the seventh-grade students left their advisories. We were all bunched up in the hallway together for just a couple of minutes before we separated again and headed for our next class. Kids were asking each other which essay topic they'd chosen and talking about how long they'd had to sit staring at their paper before they could think of a first sentence.

I passed Bradley Ryder and a few of the other A-kids just as Brad said, "Well, I guess I don't have to ask which essay question anyone here chose, huh?"

There was a lot of laughing until Melissa said, "I chose the topic on achieving world peace, of course."

Oh, of course, I thought. Melissa was sure to believe everyone was desperate to hear her ideas on the subject. She was probably hoping someone would send her essay to the U.N.

The A-kids, however, thought she was out of her mind.

"Are you crazy?" one of them asked her.

"It was a *test*," Melissa said, as if the people she was speaking to ought to have understood that without her having to tell them. "To be really tested, I had to write an essay on a new topic, not on a topic I'd written about before."

"Some of the words on the vocabulary portion of the survey we've had on tests in school over the last couple of years," Brad pointed out. "Did you not answer those because you couldn't *really* be tested on them now if you'd been tested on them before?"

"It's not the same thing," Melissa said.

"There are only so many words, and there are only so many questions. Some people are going to have seen some of these things before," Brad told her.

Even Melissa had to admit that was true. That's how logical and reasonable Brad is. He can even win over Melissa, who is not at all logical and reasonable. She's more on the bossy and know-it-all side.

She smiled and said, "I did a really good job on the world peace essay. I wish I had a copy."

I was guessing she wanted to send it to the U.N. herself.

The school schedule was all mixed up because of testing. At lunchtime I ended up having to wait in line at the cafeteria by myself, so I quickly snuck *Happy Kid!* out of my backpack and let it fall open. I'd been checking it whenever I had a chance for two weeks, but it had always opened to the "Something to Look Forward To" chapter. That probably meant that it was just an ordinary book with a bad binding that kept it from opening properly. I wanted to chuck the thing into a corner of my room. I really did. But I kept thinking, Maybe this time it will open somewhere else and have something else to say. Even though I knew that books don't actually *say* things.

Still, I kept *Happy Kid!* with me all the time and let it open up whenever I could do it without someone catching me. If the book ended up not having some kind of mystical thing going on, then it was just jerky, and I didn't want anyone seeing me with it.

There, in the cafeteria line, all my effort was finally rewarded. For no reason at all that I could see, I was face-to-face with a new chapter.

Kick-start Your Life with Something New!

Try something you've never done before. You need a jolt to get you out of the tired old ways of thinking and living that are keeping you from forming satisfying relationships and enjoying a happy life. New activities mean meeting new people, new people who might become your new best friends. The act of doing something different makes you a different person than you were before. Being a different person can only be a good thing since whatever you were before wasn't working for you, now, was it?

I smiled as I put the book back in my backpack before anyone could see it. "Kick-start." I was meeting Mr. Goldman after school later that week, so the message had to be about taekwondo. The book wanted me to take taekwondo. And since I wanted to take it, too, I was feeling very kindly toward *Happy Kid!*

It was nice to have something to feel good about during

101

the next few days as our teachers forced us to do relaxing, fun activities so we could unwind after taking tests each morning. Mrs. Haag was right. Compared to what some of the other teachers had planned, watching her sex education videos really was a treat.

Mr. Borden, for instance, made us read plays. Out loud. While standing at the front of the classroom. He said that role-playing helps people learn things and that we'd be doing theater-type activities all year long. All the A-kids cheered.

When I told my mother about "Borden's Playhouse," which was what Mr. Borden started calling his classroom during the SSASies, she got on me right away. She said I was complaining about something fun that most students would be grateful to have an opportunity to do. Okay. That *might* have been true—if Mr. Borden hadn't written the plays *himself*. They were these depressing things about people who were dead and watching their own funerals, or families sitting around a table at Thanksgiving and fighting, or adults crying in their living room because they didn't get what they wanted for Christmas.

And people say *I'm* negative.

But one day while I was at my locker, I took a minute to see if *Happy Kid!* had a new message. It didn't. It was still telling me to kick-start my life with something new. "Try something you've never done before," it said. "You need a jolt to get you out of the tired old ways of thinking and living that are keeping you from forming satisfying relationships and enjoying a happy life."

Wait right there! I thought. What if this message isn't about taekwondo at all? The book didn't have to tell me to take taekwondo. I was already signed up. If the book was supernatural, wouldn't it know I was already planning to do what it wanted me to? Maybe now it was telling me to do something else.

But what? I thought as I walked to English class.

Before I knew it, I was volunteering to read a part in one of Mr. Borden's plays. It was definitely something I'd never done before. Plus, Chelsea was in my English class. Maybe if I read a part, I would form a satisfying relationship with her and enjoy a happy life. That was what *Happy Kid!* was supposed to be about, after all.

Soon I was one of five students sitting in a semicircle in front of the class, reading from the scripts Mr. Borden gave us. I didn't miss any cues, and I don't think I pronounced any words wrong. About halfway through the play I was beginning to think that I could feel myself being jolted out of my tired old ways when Mr. Borden stopped us.

"Kyle, you don't understand the role," he told me.

That was true.

"You see, the man isn't really unhappy because he didn't receive a train when he was ten. The train is a symbol," Mr. Borden explained.

"Oh," I said. "Oh, okay."

"Do you understand what the train is a symbol for?" Mr. Borden asked.

"Come on!" Melissa said impatiently when I didn't answer. "It's a symbol for *all* the things your character wants in life."

I almost laughed because that couldn't possibly be right. Fortunately, I saw Chelsea silently nodding her head, agreeing with Melissa. She saved me, just in time, from making a total fool of myself.

Still, I had this feeling we weren't any closer to forming the satisfying relationship I'd been trying for.

Things didn't go a whole lot better with Ms. Cannon. Her idea of a restful and enjoyable activity after a long morning of answering SSASie questions was discussing a two- or three-page article about elections in foreign countries where all the candidates have long names no one can pronounce. So she assigned current events every single day instead of just on Fridays the way she usually did.

Normally I would have thought I'd be able to nail current events easy. It's in my blood. My grandmother makes sure I'm kept informed about every kidnapping, chemical spill, and terrorist event that occurs almost anywhere in the world, after all.

But, as it turns out, A-kids don't need their grandmothers to keep them informed on what's happening in the world. They get their current events directly from *Newsweek, Time, U.S. News and World Report*, and something called *The Christian Science Monitor*. They read the local newspaper every day and not just the comic section.

A-kids suck up current events the way creatures on the Sci Fi Channel suck up energy from doomed planets. And then the A-kids are stronger and more powerful. During current events days, our room looked like those scenes you see on television of the New York Stock Exchange where all these people are waving their arms, holding papers, and shouting things. Everyone wanted to be picked first in case someone else had chosen the same current event they did.

Nobody wanted to be the *second* person to talk about state representatives accepting bribes, the way I was because Melissa beat me to it. Or the second person to talk about how expensive it is to go to the state university, the way I was because Brad beat me to it. Or the second person to talk about how lack of exercise is killing people, the way I was because Chelsea beat me to it. Though Chelsea didn't beat me on purpose. She just spoke first.

I was always coming in second because it was hard for me to get up as much excitement for the news as A-kids did. I tried to jump up and down in my seat and go, "Me! Me! Me! Pick me!" But that was just not *me*. I couldn't just sit there, either, because how would that look to Chelsea? I didn't want her to think I wasn't like her, that I didn't love talking about things that had happened to people I didn't know in places I'd never been.

Then one day while I was checking out the same old "Kickstart Your Life with Something New" passage, I got an idea. Maybe *Happy Kid!* had never meant for me to use Borden's Playhouse to get out of my tired old ways that were keeping me from forming a satisfying relationship with Chelsea. Maybe it meant for me to use . . . current events.

I came up with a plan.

I got up early and went onto CNN.com just before I left for school. That meant I was getting the absolutely most recent news, news the A-kids hadn't seen because they're A-kids and had done their homework the night before the way they were supposed to. After nearly two weeks of current events, I knew certain topics to stay away from. Brad was into school stories. There was a girl in the class who always did war coverage. Melissa went for any article about corruption. Chelsea liked fitness articles. My plan was to choose something they *wouldn't* choose. Then, when I finally got a chance to speak, I would have a topic no one else had picked. It didn't even have to be a good topic because I was always chosen so late in the period that everyone expected all the good topics to be gone, anyway.

Chelsea would be so impressed.

I was feeling great when I got to class. I sat down at my desk, crossed my arms, and leaned back to relax and enjoy watching the others compete for Ms. Cannon's attention.

Then, out of the blue, like a meteor dropping out of the sky, Ms. Cannon said to me, "Kyle, you haven't had a chance to say much this week. Why don't you go first today?"

Now? I wanted to shout. Now you decide to pick me? Now when I'm *not* raising my hand and making a fool of myself jumping up and down in front of you?

That was my first thought. My second thought was, What was the topic I chose? Oh, that's right. I chose the topic no A-kid would ever want.

106

Then, while I had the complete attention of everyone in the room and could have spoken about any important thing that was going on in the entire world, I had to sit at my desk and say, "CNN.com reported this morning that yesterday a man came out of a four-year coma and asked for a Snickers bar."

There was a moment of silence—no one wanted to laugh at a current event that pathetic—then everyone turned toward Ms. Cannon, raised their hands, started hopping up and down, and shouted, "Me! Me!"

I had to grab the sides of my desk to keep myself from jumping up and screaming, Kyle! You moron! The stupid book made you kick-start your life with . . . with class participation! What good did that ever do anybody?

CHAPTER 9

☹ 😐 🙂 😐 ☹ 😐

I started taekwondo the first Tuesday in October.

The two-week SSASie testing period had ended the Friday before, so I had real homework again. I got Tuesday's done in the afternoon, then I rushed through dinner so I could take a shower and fix up my hair since that night's class would be the first time Chelsea saw me outside of school.

Oh, and I also had to make sure my feet were clean, because we train barefoot. Washing my feet a couple of times a week—as if I needed one more thing to do.

When I got into Mrs. Slocum's car around six-thirty, Luke and Ted were already in their doboks, a two-piece white uniform with a cloth belt that ties at the waist. I was carrying mine in an old gym bag. Luke looked from me to the bag and said, "Oh, Kyle, man, you don't want to use the locker room."

"Mr. Goldman showed it to me when I went for one of my introductory lessons," I said. "I thought everybody used it."

"Only the adults," Ted told me.

"You're going to have to change your clothes with old guys," Luke said. "Ick. You're going to have to undress with—"

"Yeah, I get it."

Sure enough, when I went into the locker room to change, the only person there was a heavy man with a lot of black, oily hair. He was nearly through getting into his dobok, so I made a big deal about looking for something in my gym bag until he left. Then I rushed to get dressed and was able to leave when another man arrived with an enormous black bag with a rubbery-looking helmet hanging off a strap on the outside.

Helmets? We were going to be doing something that required us to wear helmets? During one of my private lessons, Mr. Goldman had told me that after I reached the green belt rank, I could buy my own "gear"—a padded vest, ankle and wrist pads, and a mouth guard—but I was almost certain he hadn't said anything about a helmet. How could I have missed the info about having to protect myself from blows to my head?

When I left the locker room, Luke and Ted were in the middle of the spongy blue mat that covered most of the floor of the training room, which Mr. Goldman had said I had to call the dojang because in Korean that's what you call a training room. He also told me that before we stepped onto the mat in the dojang, we had to bow toward the flags hanging on the wall opposite us at the back of the room.

I just stood there for a minute because bowing is weird-looking, and I wasn't going to do it unless everyone else was.

Even when I saw that everyone else *was* doing it, I checked to see if anyone was watching me. That's how I happened to see Chelsea coming up behind me with a big black bag of gear. She had her hair up in a ponytail and she was wearing a red scrunchie that matched the red belt over her dobok. She bowed without even pausing, as if she wasn't even thinking about it, and marched across the dojang to drop her bag along the wall.

So I bowed, too.

But then what? Luke and Ted were pretending to grab at each other and then batting their hands away. Luke kept missing or getting hit because he was always looking away to see what Holly Cappa was doing. He didn't make a sound except for shouting occasionally, the way we're supposed to whenever we strike with our hands or feet.

There were ten or twelve other people on the mat, about half of them my age, and then some adults who might have been in their twenties or thirties or even older than my parents. Chelsea stood in front of one of the two walls that were covered with mirrors, put her foot in her hand, and stretched her leg straight out in front of her. Then she lifted it until her foot was as high as her shoulder. I'd never seen her do anything like that before. She looked fantastic. After she'd stretched both legs, she stood in front of the mirror with her hands up in fists. She suddenly spun around backwards, shifted her weight from one foot to the other, and brought one leg up as the rest of her body leaned away from it. Somewhere in all that she also did a kick.

110

I was still staring at her and thinking she was the most incredible girl I'd ever seen who wasn't on television and that I ought to go up to her and say hello to let her know I was there and maybe compliment her on her scrunchie or something when Mr. Goldman marched into the dojang and called, "Line up, please."

"Sir!" the others shouted as they started running to form four lines. I still had my eyes on Chelsea. She was getting into a line in the middle of the room. "New activities mean meeting new people, new people who might become your new best friends." I had read that line in *Happy Kid!* over and over again. After wasting my time reading a play out loud in English and that current events article in social studies, I'd decided that passage and everything else in that book were just meaningless words. But standing there in the dojang, I suddenly thought that I knew exactly what "new activities mean meeting new people" meant.

I rushed across the dojang to take a spot beside Chelsea. Finally, we would be next to each other. Tonight was going to be the beginning of everything I'd been waiting for and looking forward to—the ninth-grade classes we'd take as eighth-graders, walking together in the halls at the high school, the Pr—

I had almost reached her when one of the black belts signaled to me. "We line up by rank," she whispered. "You need to be over there with the other white belts."

Over there. Behind Luke and Ted, who were yellow belts because they'd passed their test at the end of September. Next to a tough-looking woman and a skinny guy who shaved his head. On the exact opposite side of the dojang.

Try something you've never done before! I thought as I rushed to the back of the dojang so that I could find my place before anyone noticed. I'm *never* doing that again.

We hadn't even got to the part of the class where Mr. Goldman made us run around the dojang six times—two of them backwards. Or the warm-up exercises that went on forever and ever. Or the ten minutes or so of just standing in lines and kicking and punching at nothing while Mr. Goldman counted in Korean. Or the crummy self-defense moves white belts had to learn. While the higher-ranked people were doing these really cool things that involved grabbing people's arms and pinning them behind their backs so that they ended up on the floor, we were learning how to slap away someone's hand if he tried to grab our belts. Which would be very useful in real life, I'm sure.

We finally got into two lines facing one another so we could practice something called step sparring. As far as I could tell, step sparring was just doing one move over and over again as the person across from you pretended to punch you. That's a whole lot of fun. The person across from me was *not* Chelsea but some green belt who was way, way too into what he was doing, what with his shouting and leaping sideways. Then Mr. Goldman told us to turn, which meant we turned to another partner by moving along the line to another person. This is it, I thought. I'm going to get to step spar with Chelsea. I can see her in the other line. We'll keep moving and sooner or later I'll get to her.

She was getting closer . . . and closer . . .

. . . and then she passed me because when we changed partners we moved *two* partners to our right, not one. I had to watch her move right past me and stop to spar with some woman brown belt.

I think she might have nodded at me as she went by, though.

"How was it?" Dad asked me when he picked us up in the parking lot after class. His voice had this sense of dread in it, as if he hated to hear what I had to say but felt he had a fatherly responsibility to show an interest.

"It was terrible, of course," I said in a low voice from the front seat while Luke and Ted sat in back and discussed how soon they could try breaking boards with their feet. In order to avoid going back into the locker room, I hadn't bothered changing out of my dobok. It was so wet with sweat that when I got outdoors, the cooler air made the cloth cold. I couldn't bring myself to lean back against it in the car, so I sat hunched forward against my seat belt.

"It's like being in the army or something. The teacher tells us where to stand and how to stand. If we don't have one of the positions just right, one of the black belts comes over and tells us 'bend your legs more' or 'keep your back foot over to the right more.' And then we just stand in lines and kick at nothing. And we have to bow to anyone with a black belt. And we have to call them all 'sir' or 'ma'am.' "

"Oh. Well, that doesn't sound *too* bad," Dad said.

"And on top of everything else, there were an odd number of white belts there, so sometimes I had to stand in front of a mirror and fight with myself."

"It won't always be that way," Luke said from the backseat. "There's some woman white belt who comes sometimes. You'll be able to train with her."

"Her daughter used to babysit for my brothers and me," Ted added.

"She's old enough to have a *daughter* who used to babysit for you?" I yelped.

"It doesn't really matter who you train with," Ted explained. "We're not supposed to talk, anyway. It's not like you're there to make friends or anything. You get to change partners off and on during the lessons. And Mr. Goldman really doesn't like it if people complain about who they have to train with. We're all supposed to be equal in the dojang."

"That's why the black belts have to help teach us and help clean the dojang after class," Luke said. "They aren't supposed to think they're better than anyone else."

"We *can't* talk? I noticed it was quiet, but I didn't think it was because we couldn't talk!" I could *not* talk to Chelsea at school. I didn't need to go to a special class to *not* talk to her.

"Can we get our money back?" I asked my father.

"Your mother signed a three-month contract."

"Three months! It will be Christmas before I can quit."

"There's going to be another testing period in December. Maybe you'll be invited to test for your yellow belt then," Luke suggested.

"Is that supposed to be something to look forward to? Being *invited* to take a *test*?" I demanded.

Dad reached over and patted my knee as if I were some kind of wild dog he was trying to calm down. Then he said, "I just want to go on record as saying I told your mother this was a bad idea."

"Doing something new is one of those things that's really overrated," I told him.

Dad nodded. "I haven't done anything new since 1991."

"I'm going to take another shower!" I shouted when I got home.

I'm going to take a shower, I'm going to take a shower, I kept thinking as I went upstairs. But when I got to my room, I didn't pick up some clean underwear and a pair of sweatpants. I picked up *Happy Kid!* I'm going to take a shower, I told myself as I balanced the spine of the book in my hand. I'm going to—

The front and back covers fell away from each other and the pages flipped open to a new chapter.

Nothing Comes Easy

Things aren't always going to go the way you expect them to. Every plan has a flaw. Everything is harder than you think it will be. There's no logical reason for this. It just is. Don't worry about it.

115

"Everything is harder than you think it will be," I read again. It couldn't be a coincidence that I was reading that line at that moment. But what good did it do me? And why tell me "There's no logical reason for this"? Wasn't the book supposed to be helpful?

What exactly is this thing? I wondered as I stood there looking at *Happy Kid!* there in my hand.

I ran out of my room and down the stairs and found my mother folding clothes in the living room.

"So, how was your first class?" she asked. Her voice had that same sense of dread in it I'd heard earlier in Dad's.

"Dad didn't tell you?"

"Well, yes, he did."

"Then you know I hate it," I said.

Mom pulled one of Lauren's bras out of a hamper of clean clothes. One of my new boxer shorts was tangled up in the straps. I so wish I hadn't seen that. "Kyle, hate is an emotion that does no one any good. You don't hate that class. You can't hate something you've only done once."

"Yeah, you're right. I just *think* I hate it."

"Reading *Happy Kid!* doesn't seem to be helping you at all. You're just as negative as you've ever been," she complained.

"Let's say I've had a setback. Where did you get that book, anyway?" I asked. "Where were you when that thing 'screamed' my name?"

"Hmm. Uh . . ."

116

She didn't seem to want to tell me. Oh, no! What had she done? Bought it at one of those incense and crystal places?

"Oh, okay. I got it at Wal-Mart," Mom suddenly admitted.

"Wal-Mart?"

"I was shopping for towels and underwear. I told you. I happened to push my cart through the book section of the store, and there it was."

That made me feel safe, at least. After all, Wal-Mart won't even sell CDs that require parental warning labels. What were the chances it would sell a book that would actually do something bad?

Now the only question left was, What was it supposed to do?

"A little stenchy, aren't you?" Lauren said to me as she passed me in the hall. She tapped my soggy dobok with one finger and then wiped it on her pants. "A shower would be a good idea right about now."

"I don't need you to tell me when to take a shower," I told her.

"Taekwondo isn't improving your personality any, that's for sure," Lauren observed.

"Wait just a minute. You don't have interests outside of school. How come Mom is always making this big stinking deal about me getting involved in something, but she doesn't say a word about you?" I demanded.

Lauren smiled. "I date," she explained as she continued on to wherever she was going.

When I woke up the next morning, my calves, thighs, and shoulders felt swollen and stiff. While Mr. Goldman had been spending way too much time making our class warm up and cool down the night before, I had been hiding behind the bald white belt and moving just enough to keep the black belts off my back. No wonder all the other people in the dojang didn't mind stretching before class.

I dragged myself to school and shuffled through the halls as fast as my suffering muscles would let me. Mr. Kowsz yelled at me in the hall for holding up traffic. He had only had his cast off his foot for a week. The entire first month of school he'd hobbled around the building, holding up traffic. Now all of a sudden *my* being slow was a problem?

I managed to get into my advisory classroom just as Mrs. Haag and some of the girls were getting started on a big discussion on . . . current events.

Mrs. Haag patted the page of the newspaper she'd been reading and said, "SSASie testing hasn't been over for a week—a week—and already somebody has been reported for cheating at an elementary school. Can you believe it?" She laughed.

"Little kids cheat all the time," Melissa complained. "They're awful. We didn't do things like that when we were their age."

"I don't think little kids cheat any more than anyone else," Jamie called from the back of the room. "They just, like, haven't had much practice, so they get caught more often."

"It wasn't a kid," Mrs. Haag explained. "It was a teacher."

"A teacher?" Melissa repeated slowly. "That's just terrible."

"It's not the first time an adult has been caught cheating or making some kind of mistake giving these types of tests," Mrs. Haag said.

"So, like, if I don't do well on the tests, it could be because you, like, made a mistake handing me the test booklets?" Beth asked.

Mrs. Haag looked at her for a moment, then said, "Probably not."

I limped to the front of the room so I could use the pencil sharpener while the four of them went on and on about all the reasons Beth might have done poorly on the tests, most of them having to do with the amount of time she spent talking on the phone and watching television. Then I limped back to my desk. Nobody cared.

It was one thing to have tried to kick-start my life and have my plan not go the way I'd expected it to. It was another thing altogether to be in physical pain because of it.

"Were you sore like this after your first taekwondo class?" I asked Luke when I got to art.

"Oh, yeah. I didn't do many of the warming-up and cooling-down exercises they told us to do," Luke said. "I meant to warn you about that."

"Is there anything else you forgot to tell me?" I groaned as I tried to get settled on my stool.

"You'll like it better when we do real sparring," Luke promised. "It's practice fighting. You get to kick and punch at some-

119

one, but you can't actually touch him unless your training partner is wearing chest protection."

"Play fighting?" Jake broke in. "You do play fighting there?"

"We practice," Luke repeated.

"You dress up in special outfits," Jake said. "That's playing."

"Okay," Luke said. "Some of the people at our school play that they're fighting with knives and sticks, too."

"Knives? Really?" I exclaimed.

"Well, they're made of wood," Luke admitted. "But you learn how to disarm someone who is attacking you with one of them."

"Will we be doing that soon?" I asked hopefully.

"In a year or so, I think," Luke replied. "You have to be a red belt before they teach you that."

"Hope nobody attacks you with a knife before then," Jake said as he went to work on one of the dirty cartoons he liked to draw in class. "Especially a real one."

Chelsea was a red belt. That meant she'd be learning the knife stuff soon. She was so cool.

I was almost glad I was taking taekwondo because Luke and I would have something to talk about now besides all the movies he was seeing without me. Then I thought, Hey, I could talk with Chelsea about taekwondo. Not during our taekwondo classes, but here at school.

In fact, I wondered if maybe that was what *Happy Kid!* had meant when it said things wouldn't always go the way I expect them to. I could still use taekwondo to form a satisfying relationship with her. Only not at the dojang the way I'd planned.

Okay, then. If that was what *Happy Kid!* was telling me I should do, I had to think of a way to get a conversation started with Chelsea. How hard could that be? I just needed to get to social studies early so I'd have a chance to talk to her before class started.

Even moving as slowly as I was, I got to social studies in plenty of time. I was actually heading across the room toward Chelsea's desk when I noticed Ms. Cannon was looking at me.

I assumed she was going to start talking about graduate school because she hadn't mentioned it in days and was overdue. Imagine my surprise when instead she said to me, "Are you okay?"

"Oh, I'm fine. Fine," I said as I kept walking. "I started taekwondo last night, and I guess I overdid it."

"Oh, really?" Ms. Cannon said. "What got you interested in that?"

I couldn't believe it. She always chose the worst possible time to pay attention to me.

Then I realized that if I started talking taekwondo with Ms. Cannon, it would be really logical for Chelsea to get involved with the conversation, too. So I stopped where I was and said to Ms. Cannon, "I got interested because I have friends who study taekwondo." Just to make sure I'd said enough to get a discussion going, I added, "I'm working on a yellow belt."

It worked. Ms. Cannon was interested. She said, "So what *is* taekwondo, anyway?"

"Um, you know, it's a martial art. Master Lee uses it in his movies," I explained.

"Oh, I don't watch *those*," she said with this little laugh, as if maybe I shouldn't have brought that up. "Isn't there a philosophy behind taekwondo? What is that about?"

A philosophy? Things definitely weren't going the way I expected them to, because I didn't even know what *philosophy* was.

"Don't you take taekwondo, Chelsea?" Melissa asked, butting in to a conversation that had nothing to do with her.

"Yes," Chelsea said, smiling. "I've been training since I was in third grade."

Ms. Cannon turned toward her. "How does that work? Do you get different colored belts as you get better?"

"That's right. You start off as a white belt and move up through yellow, a couple of greens, a couple of blues, a couple of reds. Then you get to brown and black."

"What belt do you have?" one of the kids asked.

"Red."

Ms. Cannon said, "You're really right up there!"

What was I supposed to say then? I'm a white belt! You just don't get any lower than that, right, Chelsea? It didn't seem like something that would keep me in the discussion for very long.

They were just getting started on how Chelsea was about to start learning how to disarm attackers who were holding knives when I slouched back to my desk. Chelsea was having a conversation about taekwondo, just as I'd expected her to. It just wasn't a conversation that involved me.

Just like *Happy Kid!* said: "Every plan has a flaw." I wondered if maybe the passages in the book weren't advice but warnings and I just didn't get them.

CHAPTER 10

☹ 😐 ☺ 😐 ☹ 😐

On a Thursday morning more than a week before Halloween, I decided to check out *Happy Kid!* while I was on the bus. I had let it open that morning right after I got up and again when I finished in the bathroom, but the book kept flipping to the same "Nothing Comes Easy" chapter I'd been seeing for more than two weeks. I really didn't have much hope that anything would happen on the bus, but I didn't want to spend the whole ride to school reading ahead in my copy of *The Odyssey,* either. So I pulled *Happy Kid!* out of my backpack and let it fall open.

There it was, a new message.

Say Yes to New Opportunities!

There are lots of opportunities all around you for great experiences with great people. But you'll never get a chance to take advantage of them if your mind is closed to anything new. If you automatically say no to everything new and different, you'll be spending a lot of time at home, where everything is old and the same. Say yes to new opportunities.

New opportunities? I thought. There is no way I'm going to like this.

Sure enough, the first new opportunity came up in English class.

"We'll be coming to the end of *The Odyssey* soon," Mr. Borden announced at the beginning of class, which was a huge relief as far as I was concerned. "We should be finishing in two to three weeks. It will be time, then, for another presentation here at Borden's Playhouse."

Some girls clapped their hands. Even a couple of the boys looked excited. I thought I should try to show some A-kid-type enthusiasm, just in case Chelsea was looking my way, so I managed a weak "Oh. Yay. Borden's Playhouse."

Then Mr. Borden asked, "Who wants to be part of the creative team behind 'Scenes from *The Odyssey*'?"

If Chelsea volunteered, I would, too. I didn't have a clue what we'd have to do, but if Chelsea was on a creative team, I was going to be there with her.

Slowly, smoothly, Chelsea's hand went up. My arm shot up with a snap. (It felt a lot like a perfect taekwondo punch, as a matter of fact, though in a totally wrong direction.)

" . . . Melissa and . . . oh, Kyle," Mr. Borden said, sounding surprised. "Very good. So that's Emily, Gillian, Phil, Melissa, and Kyle. That should be enough."

I looked away from Chelsea to Melissa. Melissa looked away from Mr. Borden to me. I hoped the expression on my face wasn't half as disappointed as the one on hers. A *quarter*, even.

A second opportunity *almost* came up at lunch.

It being Thursday and all, I had hoped someone at lunch would mention going to the movies Friday night and there would be an opportunity for me to say, "Yeah, I guess I could meet you there." That was a really, really positive thing for me to be thinking.

But instead of making plans to go to the movies the next night, Luke started talking about Halloween, which wasn't for another week.

Ted said to him, "You know what I was thinking we should do for Halloween? We should use our doboks for costumes."

"Yes!" Luke exclaimed. "That will look cool—especially now that we have yellow belts to wear with them."

"What are you guys doing for Halloween?" I asked, trying to sound as if I really wasn't paying too much attention to the conversation.

"This girl in our English class asked us to a party," Luke said. "I don't think you know her," he added awkwardly. "You're in accelerated English, you know."

I knew.

Oh, this is a great opportunity, I thought. An opportunity for everyone to know that I'm alone—again—on Halloween. For everyone to see that no one wants to be with me.

While those thoughts were going through my mind, I heard someone say, "I don't know what I'll be doing on Halloween. I haven't made up my mind yet."

That someone was me.

Everyone around me started talking about what they were doing on Halloween. Hearing all their plans didn't bother me nearly as much as I thought it would because I was just so glad that they were talking about something, anything, and not silently wondering what was wrong with Kyle.

The third opportunity came later in the afternoon.

I got to science class and in walked Jake, who came up to me and said, "Hey, you're not going to this kid Halloween party little Lukie's going to, are you? Tell me you're too cool for that."

"I'm too cool. Way too cool," I told him.

"Good. Why don't you come out with Brian, Kenny, and me? We're going to hang out at the mall. You can be part of my posse."

No, no, no. This was an opportunity to do something new and different, and I was saying *no* to it. I didn't care what kind of message *Happy Kid!* was trying to give me. I was not hanging out at the mall with Jake.

"We might go in some kind of costumes, but we haven't decided yet," Jake continued. "We're going to hit the Mexican place at the food court, and then go into some nice stores and fart in the changing rooms. We've done that before. It is hysterical. You don't know any girls you'd like to invite, do you?

It would be really funny if we could get a girl to gas up at the food court with us and then head on into the women's changing rooms."

Jake couldn't find a girl on his own to "gas up at the food court" with him? Why wasn't I surprised?

"Ah, that sounds great. I'm not going to be able to make it, though," I said.

"Why not? You going out trick-or-treating?" Jake sneered.

"Ah, no, no, of course not. Haven't done that in a while," I said, trying to buy some time while I came up with a good excuse. Behind Jake's back I could see Luke staring at me and silently mouthing a word. He had to do it a few times before I picked up on his meaning.

"Taekwondo," I said to Jake finally. "I have to go to tae-kwondo class that night."

"On Halloween?"

"Hey, martial artists don't care about Halloween," I told him. "They're going to be training that night just like any other Friday night."

Oh, no. Halloween *is* on a Friday this year, I realized. I just told someone I was going to spend Halloween *and* a Friday night at the dojang. It sounded a lot like a nerd twofer to me.

"They have classes six days a week," Luke broke in. "Kyle needs to go to some extra classes because . . . he's not very good."

Thanks for the help, Luke.

"So, that's why I can't go with you," I said to Jake. "Thanks anyway."

I was used to having bad days when things didn't go my way and nothing came easy. And that particular bad day probably wasn't much worse than any other. I was just getting so tired of them, though.

When I got to the dojang that night, I was way past caring if people saw me stretching, punching at myself in front of the mirror, or standing on my head. I warmed up and then practiced my roundhouse kick in front of the mirror. Turn. Kick. Turn. Kick. Turn. Kick. I saw Chelsea's reflection in the glass. Turn. Kick.

Then I went through the moves for the poomse, or form I was learning. It was a series of punches, kicks, and blocks that I had to memorize. Low block. Punch. Low block. Turn. I could see Chelsea out of the corner of my eye practicing something with an older girl. Low block. Punch.

"Line up, please," Mr. Goldman called.

"Sir!" I shouted and ran to my place.

"Ten jumping jacks!"

"Hana!" I shouted with the others, counting in Korean each time our arms went up into the air.

"Follow me, Paul," Mr. Goldman said to the highest-ranking black belt in the room. The rows of people fell into place behind Mr. Goldman as he led us in a run around the dojang. When we were done, the long line that had snaked around the big room immediately broke up and silently re-arranged itself into three rows, three people across, for warm-up and drills.

How much longer do I have to do this? I wondered as we

started the drills. Punch. Shout. Punch. Shout. Punch. Shout. Why don't they have a clock in the front of the room? Palm strike. Shout. Palm strike. Shout. My fingers should be together. Shout. Kick. Shout. Kick. Shout. I want that foot higher. Shout. Bring the knee up and then straighten the leg. Shout. Higher. Shout. Switch stance. I can do that faster next time. Kick. Shout. Kick. Shout. Higher. Harder. Louder.

We did self-defense training that night and then lined up in front of the heavy bag for another kicking drill. I was bouncing on the balls of my feet, keeping everything loose and ready to move when I noticed Chelsea was somewhere ahead of me and realized that I'd lost track of her earlier in the class. Then I had to look away from her and toward the bag. I had to keep my hands up to guard my face. I had to guard my chest. I had to turn on my left foot, bend to my left so my body was parallel to the floor, bring my leg up, and kick the bag. The next time I came through the line I hit the bag harder. The next time I hit it at a higher spot. Harder. Higher. Harder. Higher. I just kept coming through the line toward that bag, over and over and over again.

"Line up!" Mr. Goldman shouted.

"Sir!" I shouted back with the rest of the class as I ran to get into line for the cool-down stretching.

Suddenly, we were through with even that.

"Charyot!" Mr. Goldman called, and we stood at attention.

"Kyungye!" We bowed.

"Kamsahamnida. Thank you for training this evening."

"Kamsahamnida," we all replied.

The class was over, and my mind was empty. There was just nothing in it. Probably this was because I hadn't been able to think of anything but the moves I had to make for the better part of fifty minutes. For that whole time all I'd been able to do was move. I didn't think about being the guy everyone believed had pulled a weapon on a school bus. I didn't think about being the guy who sat next to Jake Rogers in so many classes. I didn't even think about being a B-minus guy who wanted an A-plus girl to like him. As I left the dojang, I wasn't that other guy. He didn't exist there.

On the way home in the back of Ted's dad's car, I relaxed back against my seat and thought, Yes, I'll keep coming here for a while.

CHAPTER 11

☹ 🙁 ☺ 😐 ☹ 🙁

A week later I suddenly realized I had plans for Halloween. Halloween was the very next day, and I had a place to go. This year I wasn't going to be stuck staying home with my parents, pretending I was having a good time handing out candy. I was going to taekwondo. Taekwondo, where, on Tuesday night, I had kicked the stuffing out of a target. Really, little bits of fluff were floating all around the person holding it for me. Where else can a guy kick something so hard, he knocks the insides out of it and the adults watching him tell him he's doing a great job? Who knew I would be so good at this?

I didn't even mind that Luke and Ted weren't going to be there. You aren't supposed to talk, anyway, so it doesn't matter if you don't have any friends at the dojang. It might be the perfect place for me.

I was definitely feeling good in advisory the next morning, even though Friday was current events day in social studies again, and I was hunting through that day's newspaper for an article to bring to class. A short article, of course, because the A-kids always went for the long ones.

Then Melissa arrived.

The first thing she did was start badgering me.

"It's been over a week since Mr. Borden gave us the 'Scenes from *The Odyssey*' assignment. Do you know what we're supposed to do?" she asked.

"Don't you?" I replied.

"Of course I do. I spoke to Mr. Borden before class yesterday."

"Are you going to make me guess?" I asked her. "It would go a lot faster if you just told me."

"Mr. Borden wants us to adapt scenes from *The Odyssey* into short plays and then act out the parts for the class."

"We have to write plays? Well, it could be worse, I suppose," I had to admit. "Mr. Borden could be writing them."

"I picked five scenes I think would work best, and I've assigned one to each of the five people on the team. Yours is the scene where Odysseus meets the Cyclops."

"What if I don't want that scene?" I asked.

"I gave you the easiest one! How can you not want it?"

She gave me the easiest scene? She thought I needed the easiest scene? I could have pitched a fit about that, but I was afraid Melissa would take the easiest scene back and give me a hard one.

"I do want it. I like the Cyclops. I don't blame him for hating Odysseus. I hate him, too."

While we were talking, I glanced at a headline that read

"Elderly Woman Trapped in Car for Two Days." The article that accompanied it had only three short paragraphs. Perfect, I thought as I tore it out of its page.

"We're all going to have to act out parts in each other's play," Melissa said as I opened my backpack and started sliding the rest of the newspaper into it. "I suppose it's too much to expect you to memorize anything."

My backpack was full, and I had to jiggle it and poke at things a bit in order to get the paper in nice and flat. Something slid out and landed on the floor. Melissa bent down to pick it up. "Oh, what have we here? I can't believe it. You're reading a self-help book."

I couldn't believe it, either. Once again something had fallen out of my backpack and was going to get me into trouble.

"*A Young Person's Guide to Satisfying Relationships and a Happy and Meaning-Filled Life!*" Melissa read aloud as I tried to grab the book away from her. "This is sad. Really sad."

Melissa Esposito felt sorry for me. My father was wrong. You could die of embarrassment.

"That book isn't what you think it is," I said.

She held it out to me as if it were something dirty. "Of course it's not."

How long would it be before every A-kid in seventh grade knew Kyle Rideau was so miserable, he had to resort to reading a book for help? I wondered. When would Chelsea find out?

Then I noticed something just a little bit odd.

When Melissa picked *Happy Kid!* up off the floor, she only grabbed the front of the book. Her fingers were actually in between a couple of pages.

"Ah, Melissa, open the book to the page where your fingers are," I said. "Read the beginning of the new chapter your hand is touching."

I caught her off guard with that request.

"Why?" she asked.

"Just take a look at it and tell me what it says," I told her.

Melissa always does what she's told. It's a very bad habit. "Listen to Others Sometimes," she read out loud. "You might want to hear what they have to say just in case you're mistaken and you don't actually know it all. Perhaps your problems forming satisfying relationships have something to do with the way you treat—"

"That's enough," I said, stopping her from going on.

"Already read that part, Kyle?" Melissa asked.

"No. I've never seen that page before. But I think I might understand what it means," I said slowly. "Close the book, Melissa. Close it without marking your place. Leave the bound edge of the book in your hand just like you've got it there, and let the pages fall open by themselves. Now read the page that showed up."

"Listen to Others Sometimes. You might want to hear what they have to say just in—"

I snatched the book away from her. "All done. I'll take this back now."

"What was that all about?" Melissa asked.

I finally got it. But she didn't. She thought *Happy Kid!* was just a regular self-help book for a kid who needed to help himself. And that, I was afraid, was what she would tell people.

"Watch this," I told her.

I held the book in my hand just the way she had so it would open by itself. It opened to the first new chapter I'd seen in over a week.

Enjoy Surprises! That's What They're There For!

Just because you didn't expect something to happen, it doesn't follow that that something is bad. In fact, it could be good. Recognize those good surprises when they happen. Have fun with them.

"Oh!" I said when I finished reading. "It sounds as if I'm going to get a surprise."

"That's not what it sounds like to me," Melissa replied.

I shut the book with a snap and let it fall open again.

"Look! It fell open to the same place." I closed and opened the book again. "And it opened to the same place again." I closed and opened the book over and over again. Every time it opened, it opened to the same place—"Enjoy Surprises! That's What They're There For!"

I closed the book and handed it to Melissa.

"Now you let it fall open," I ordered.

She did, looked down, gasped, and closed the book again.

"You see," I said, "this isn't a regular self-help book at all.

It doesn't give sappy advice like 'listen to your parents because they're your best friends' or 'be nice and share your cookies.' It gives readers messages that are just for them."

I smiled, trying to look really creative and fascinating so that Melissa would think I was like the artistic loner in a teen movie instead of the one who dresses funny and brings his lunch from home. I could tell from the look on her face that it wasn't working.

I stopped smiling and shifted to a less pleasant plan. Telling her the truth. "If you let the book fall open to where the book wants to fall open, you'll find a chapter that has something to do with what is going on in your life."

"The word for that is 'coincidence,' Kyle. I hope you had it as a vocab word sometime in your past. It means 'two unrelated events that just happen to occur at the same time.' "

"It's not a coincidence if the two unrelated events happen at the same time over and over again."

"You're reading too much into those messages of yours. They're like horoscopes or fortune cookies. They mean what you want them to mean," Melissa said. And she sneered while she was saying it.

I shoved *Happy Kid!* at her. "Try again."

"Okay," she said after she looked down at the open book. "I am seeing that same 'Listen to Others Sometimes' passage. Oooo. Spooky. The thing is, it doesn't have anything to do with me."

"Oh, come on! The book all but said you're a know-it-all. You'll never make me believe no one has ever called you that before. Don't worry," I concluded as Melissa started to object. "I won't tell anyone what your message was. Unless someone finds out about the book and says something to me about it, of course."

"You're trying to blackmail me," Melissa said, way too calmly for someone who was about to give in to blackmail. "That's really clever. I didn't think you were smart enough to do something like that. Okay. I won't tell anyone you're a loser who's trying to improve his pathetic life by reading a book. For now. But if I feel I need to sometime in the future, I will."

"Now *you're* trying to blackmail *me*," I pointed out.

"And succeeding," Melissa said as she turned to walk back to her desk.

I hoped that Melissa agreeing to keep her mouth shut for a while wasn't the good surprise *Happy Kid!* had been talking about. I had been hoping for something better.

I got a math test back first period with a big red C at the top of it. No surprise there. Jake got thrown out of art class for the first time for making body function jokes. That was only surprising because it had taken Mr. Ruby so long to do it.

When I got to social studies third period, I wasn't expecting any surprises. It was current events day, after all, and current events day is always the same. I spend most of the period waiting for everyone else to get tired of talking so I can get a chance to say something. I was so certain nothing unexpected would happen that I didn't even listen particularly closely to what the A-kids were saying. I couldn't help but notice Melissa's current event discussion, though, because in addition to knowing everything, she's kind of loud about it. And she's obsessed with stories about politicians and businesspeople committing crimes at work or cheating on their taxes. According to her, that sort of thing happens *all the time* and it is *just plain wrong*. Well, okay.

So I was just sitting there wondering about whether or not my mother had remembered to throw my dobok in the washer before she went to work when Brad started to speak. Like all A-kids, he went on and on for a while and then all of a sudden he said something that sounded like, "Blah blah blah blah blah *test scores for accelerated and honors courses* blah blah blah."

"What?" I exclaimed. "What test scores? What courses?" Had he said "accelerated courses" the way I thought he had?

"Weren't you listening?" Melissa complained.

Brad gave me a summary without acting as if I must be brain-dead not to have picked up on what was going on when he talked about it the first time. "The point of the article is that some teachers in our state want the SSASies revised so they're easier to give to students. Test scores have had to be thrown out several times because teachers made mistakes giving the instructions or used the wrong kind of materials to help students prepare for them. The test results have to be accurate because a lot of schools use them to identify students who need extra help and should go to summer school or to identify students who are doing really well and should take more challenging courses the next year."

"But Mrs. Haag said the tests were for the schools, not the students," Melissa objected.

"They are," Ms. Cannon said. "But once the schools have all these scores on student achievement for the different subjects, they can use them for the students individually as well as for the schools as a whole. So a lot of school systems use the results to place students when the kids move from one school to another within the school system."

"From middle school to high school, for instance," Brad added.

I was definitely getting the picture. "So next year we'd better be really careful when we take the SSASies, huh?" I said.

"I hope you were careful when you took them *this* year," Ms. Cannon replied. "Those scores will be used to determine whether or not you can take any of the ninth-grade courses the high school offers for eighth-graders."

That wasn't a good surprise. I thought I was just going to automatically move on with Chelsea next year to those courses. I had to take a test to be with her?

I managed to casually glance around the room to see how everyone else was taking the news. There were some nervous laughs and a few people were making faces. And Melissa looked as if she really regretted not choosing the "Are we alone?" essay topic.

I tried to look as if I didn't have a care in the world, but all the time I was thinking, Sure, I always get good scores on the SSASies. But just how well do you have to do to get into those ninth-grade classes?

After another bad day at school, I was looking forward to taekwondo that evening. But by the time I finished warming up and practicing my form, only five more people had arrived, all blue belts or higher, with me being the only person under thirty or so.

I was busy trying not to be negative about having to spend Halloween with old people who were all better at taekwondo than I was when I heard the door to the men's locker room opening up behind me. Mr. Goldman nodded at whoever had just come into the dojang. I looked over my shoulder to see if it was someone I recognized.

A figure wearing a black belt over his white dobok was bowing before walking onto the mat. He straightened up, took one step forward, saw me, and stopped. Then he came toward me with his hand out. He had to come all the way to me because I couldn't move.

The look of shock on Mr. Kowsz's face as we shook hands would have been really funny if I hadn't been so sure that I was wearing one just like it on mine. We bowed to one another. Neither one of us had expected this to happen.

CHAPTER 12

☹ ☺ ☺ ☺ ☹ ☺

Mr. Kowsz was a black belt at *my* dojang, the place where *I* liked to go. Was that a good surprise because—

No! There was no possible way it could be good. I was not being negative. I was not looking for the worst in life. Facts were facts. Because of Mr. Kowsz, everyone thought I was some kind of kid criminal. Now he was bringing all that into the dojang. *My* dojang.

"Line up!" Mr. Goldman called after we'd all run around the room a few times.

"Sir!" I shouted.

"Ten jumping jacks!"

"Hana!" I yelled as I began jumping. "Dul!"

All through the warm-up, my head kept twitching to my left so I could try to see what Mr. Kowsz was doing. He was always staring straight ahead and following Mr. Goldman's instructions.

"Fighting stance! Front kick! Hana!"

I kicked and kicked and kicked and then switched stances and kicked some more.

After the drills, we worked on our forms for a while. My turns became spins that sent me stumbling, so I couldn't move in a straight line the way I was supposed to, and my upward blocks looked as if I was waving. I was ready to move on to something else long before Mr. Goldman ordered all the students to put on their gear for sparring practice.

Everyone ran to their bags and started pulling out padded vests and helmets and shin, wrist, and mouth guards. Since I was the only person there whose rank was so low that he didn't own any protective gear, I had to just stand there doing nothing. So I couldn't help noticing all the guys putting on big plastic cups *over* their doboks. They were held in place with wide elastic bands around their waists and between their legs for all the world to see.

I tried not to stare.

"Kyle and Tim!" Mr. Goldman called.

I called out "Sir!" and ran over to him.

"I'd like the two of you to train together. Kyle doesn't have any kind of protective gear yet," Mr. Goldman explained to someone coming up behind me. Then he turned to me. "And this is Tim's first class in nearly four months because of a foot injury. So you two start out together. Take it easy on each other."

I sighed, turned, and put my hand out so I could shake

hands with Mr. Kowsz. His helmet didn't make him look any better.

Mr. Goldman ordered the others to find partners and line up across from them. "You're going to start out with kicking only, light contact to chest protection if your partner has it. No contact at all to anyone who doesn't have chest protection. That pretty much means no kicking Kyle. One-minute round. Fighting stance! Begin!"

I was the only person without chest protection. That didn't sound good. But while I was trying to figure out what I should be doing about it, "Tim's" right leg came up, twisted, and headed right toward me in a roundhouse kick. And then it stopped in midair just an inch or two from my ribs.

"You need to be in fighting stance," he told me.

I just stood there staring at him. He had his fists up—one guarding his chin, one his chest—and his right leg was pulled back a bit. He was bouncing up and down, moving all the time.

"Fighting stance," he repeated. "Get your fists up."

"Oh, yeah. Right."

I didn't want him to think I didn't know what fighting stance was, so as I moved into the correct position, I started to say, "I know—"

But I was cut off because Mr. Kowsz suddenly spun so his back was toward me. He looked over his shoulder, brought up a leg, and shot his foot out toward my chest. I gasped and stared at the foot that stopped just before hitting me.

He whirled back into fighting stance and patted his vest.

"Your turn," he said.

What could I do? I only knew a few kicks. I was afraid a straightforward front kick would catch him in the crotch. Even though he was wearing that protective cup (I couldn't wait for Chelsea to see me with one of those), my gut feeling was a kick to the groin was probably a huge mistake. I didn't have time to think about all this! All the other students were dashing at each other and kicking and twisting and shouting. I had to do something. Another roundhouse kick was my best bet. I brought up my leg, pivoted on my left foot so that my knee was no longer pointing forward but to my left, and swung my foot toward Mr. Kowsz's chest.

The entire top of my foot hit him at full speed. He went toppling over backwards and landed so that his hands hit the mat first with his chin tucked so that he was looking at his feet. He shouted when he hit the floor.

I stood there for a second with my hand over my mouth. Then I started to kneel down next to him. Before I could get all the way down, Mr. Kowsz was passing me on his way back up to his feet.

"Are you okay?" I asked, looking up at him. "Are you okay? Oh my gosh . . ."

Mr. Goldman was already next to us. "Continue training," he ordered the rest of the class. "Tim, is the foot okay?"

"Yeah, it's fine. He's just got an incredible kick," Mr. Kowsz said, nodding down at me because I was still kneeling on the floor.

"Light contact," Mr. Goldman told me. "Taekwondo is all

145

about control. You can't just wildly kick and swing at people. It's dangerous to do that here, and it won't do you any good if you really have to defend yourself somewhere else."

"I don't know how that happened," I said as I started to stand up.

"You need to know how everything happens when you're training here. Now, you're new, so I won't make you do push-ups for losing control like that," Mr. Goldman explained. "Instead, I'll let Tim handle this situation. Stop! Get ready for next round!" he suddenly shouted to the other students.

Mr. Kowsz signaled for me to come closer. "Just be calm. There's nothing to be upset about."

I opened my mouth to shout "I'm not upset!" but shut it again without saying anything.

"Okay, now, kick me again the way you just did, but do it very, very slowly," he ordered.

I did, and when my foot got close enough, Mr. Kowsz said, "Now tap my vest." And I did that, too.

"Now do it again," Mr. Kowsz told me. "And again . . . again . . . now faster . . . faster."

When I had tapped his vest over and over again after kicking at different speeds, he said, "Isn't your leg beginning to hurt?"

"Well . . . yeah."

"Then stop. The point of repeating a motion is to create muscle memory. You want your body to be able to do things without your mind having to think about it. You don't want to repeat the same motion to the point that you hurt yourself. Switch legs."

So I did, and we started the whole thing over again. The others switched partners and did other moves. But there I was, doing the same stupid thing over and over. And just when Mr. Kowsz said we could get back in line with the others, Mr. Goldman announced that we were done. He also said we had to help our training partners undo their vests, so I had to untie the straps that crisscrossed behind Mr. Kowsz's shoulders and a second set at his waist. What a treat that was.

Later, while the black belts mopped the mats and a brown belt vacuumed the entry, I got stuck emptying the trash from the bathroom and both the locker rooms.

Happy Halloween!

I got home, picked up a fistful of candy from the bowl by the door, and ran to my room to look at *Happy Kid!* Just as I thought, it was time for a new message.

Get Over Yourself

Didn't your mother ever tell you that you are not the center of the universe? She should have. No wonder you have trouble forming satisfying relationships. Try to remember you're not the only person in the world with problems, okay? Get over yourself.

Well, that makes no sense at all, I thought as I tossed the book into a corner of my room. So other people have problems. Does that change the fact that I have them? No, it does not.

I picked up a pair of sweatpants and a T-shirt from the floor and headed into the bathroom for a shower.

I made the very, very big mistake of telling my father that Mr. Kowsz had suddenly appeared in my taekwondo class and that I'd given Moo a kick that had sent him flying. I then had to spend the whole weekend listening to Dad's stories of his bad experiences with sports. And he had a lot of them. Which I guess shows that I'm not the only person in the world who has problems, though you'd think he'd have gotten over his by now.

When my grandmother showed up Sunday afternoon, I asked her if things had been as bad as Dad made them out to be. She said they were worse.

"And people wonder why I stick to yoga," Lauren said. "I can do it by myself and not have to listen to other people's complaints." She was lying on the couch with a bag of pretzels on her stomach and her chemistry book (her best subject, to the whole family's surprise) propped against her bent knees. This was as close to being in a yoga position as anyone had ever seen her.

"When have you ever done yoga?" I asked.

"That reminds me." She turned her head so Mom and Dad would be able to hear her. "I'd like a yoga mat and a yoga tape for Christmas!" she shouted. "And I guess I'll need some yoga workout clothes. Unless you're going to get me a car, of course."

Our living room opens onto the dining room, so we could see Mom bring a stack of plates to the table and start placing them in front of each of the chairs. She ignored Lauren and jumped right on me—as usual. "I don't think your experience Friday night at taekwondo was all that bad. You did knock an older man over, a man who had just recovered from an injury of some sort. They were pretty nice to you, all things considered. I hope you apologized."

"Don't you get it?" I protested as my father came into the living room and grabbed some pretzels from Lauren's bag. "Everything was ruined *before* I knocked Mr. Kowsz on his butt. Except for the kids from school, no one at the dojang had ever seen me before I walked in the door. I was just another student—a student who showed up on time and kicked well. That was all I had to do to make them like me. I didn't even have to talk to anybody."

"Why will any of that change?" Nana asked from one of the good living room chairs.

Lauren threw a pretzel at me. "He's afraid Moo will tell all his little friends at the doojingle or whatever they call it the sad story of Kyle and the screwdriver. Then everyone will know that he's a junior terrorist and think he's going to use his newly learned martial arts skills for evil instead of good. Am I right?"

Everyone was looking at me. I hate that. Even when it's my own family. Sometimes especially when it's my own family.

"Well . . . you know . . . maybe . . . sort of—"

"Ah, the screwdriver," Nana sighed.

"You didn't do anything wrong, Kyle," Dad said with his mouth full. "We've told you so over and over again."

Then Mom said, "You've been upset about the screwdriver so long, it's as if your anger has control of you now."

Dad, Nana, and Lauren all rolled their eyes at her because she was using family-counselor talk in the house again.

"Well, it is," Mom insisted, sounding as if she was losing a little control herself.

"I suppose you all just think . . . just think . . . I should get over myself or something?" I sputtered.

"Actually, I think that's exactly what Mom was trying to say," Lauren said, while the rest of my relatives nodded their agreement. "Get some control and move the hell on so the rest of us don't have to listen to this anymore."

On Monday morning I was actually happy to go back to school. Well, "happy" is probably not the right word. Since my relatives thought I was a whiner, I figured I might as well be at school.

I wasn't in any hurry to tell Luke about Mr. Kowsz taking taekwondo. It was too depressing. I wouldn't have had much of a chance to talk about it during art, anyway. Jake spent a big chunk of the period telling us all about how he and his buddies were followed by a security person at the mall Halloween night. He was really excited about it.

Then Luke said there were only three guys at the Halloween party he'd gone to, and he and Ted were two of them. All the girls wanted to do, he told us, was talk and listen to music, and either Beth or Jamie spilled grape soda down the back of his dobok. He didn't know for certain because they both denied it, but it had to be one of them. They were right behind him with cans of soda when it happened.

I felt better when I left art since it seemed like maybe I wasn't the only person who'd had a bad time on Halloween.

I was heading down the hall toward the cafeteria after fourth period when I ran into Mr. Kowsz chasing a couple of guys out of a boys' room. I started to just rush past him, but then, at the last minute, I turned around and said, "I didn't apologize for knocking you down the other night. I *am* sorry."

He stopped and gave me that creepy skeleton grin of his. "Now that I know you can kick like that, I'll never let it happen again."

That went really well. So I said, "Did you hurt your foot in class?"

He nodded. "In a black belt class right after school got out last June. We were sparring, and I collided with the person I was training with that night."

"The other guy get hurt?"

"She was a woman," Mr. Kowsz admitted. "A big one, though. Her foot was black and blue for a few weeks afterward, but that's all. I got the worst of it."

He looked down at his own feet for a moment and kept talking. "I don't know how it happened. Usually I don't have any trouble concentrating in class. The moves are so complicated, it pretty much knocks everything else out of my mind."

"That happens to me, too!"

151

"But I was involved with that school board inquiry about the incident on the bus last year, and because of that, I had to take a computer class at a community college and change some plans for a trip I was supposed to take with one of my kids. What with one thing and another, I couldn't keep my mind clear," Mr. Kowsz sighed.

"Oh, wow. I'm sorry," I said again.

"Ah, it was nobody's fault. Things don't always go the way you expect them to."

"Yeah," I agreed. "I guess . . . I guess you can't get down on the whole world when those things happen."

Mr. Kowsz nodded. "That's right. Well, you'd better get going, Kyle. You're going to miss lunch. But first—when do you go to taekwondo classes?"

"Tuesday and Thursday nights."

He flinched. "Part of my black belt training involves helping with a class one hour a week. I've just been assigned Thursday nights, and sometimes I'm going to have to fill in for one of the other black belts on Tuesdays. Is that going to be okay with you? I'd rather not have the people there know we've had some trouble between us. I've been going there for years. At the dojang I'm just Tim a Black Belt. Except for those years when I was Tim a Brown Belt or Tim a Blue Belt, or whatever I was, of course." He smiled and lowered his voice. "I have never been Moo there."

"Oh, no! Don't tell them anything! I want to just be Kyle a White Belt, too. Or Kyle a Yellow Belt or Kyle a Green Belt. You know. Whatever."

"Okay," Mr. Kowsz said, sounding relieved. He patted my shoulder. "Go get some lunch. I've got to go check another one of the boys' rooms, anyway."

I rushed off to the cafeteria. I had taekwondo back. Now all I wanted was to get into some of those ninth-grade courses so I could be with Chelsea in eighth grade. If I could just manage that, my life might not stink.

CHAPTER 13

☹ 😐 🙂 😐 ☹ 😐

"I told you so," I whispered to Luke and Ted when Tim the Black Belt stepped out of the men's locker room into the dojang at the beginning of that Thursday's class.

They hadn't believed me when I told them that Mr. Kowsz was a black belt and that he trained at our school. All during warm-up they kept staring at him. Then Mr. Goldman yelled at them because they weren't concentrating, and they got down to work.

About halfway through the class we broke into two groups and formed lines in front of long punching bags that were weighted on the bottom like those kids' toys that pop back up when you hit them. These bags were a whole lot harder to knock over, though. And if you did, they didn't come back up.

I know because I did it.

When Mr. Goldman told us to form two lines, I came *this close* to getting into the wrong one. Then I noticed that everyone under eighteen was in the other group. I just managed to join them before we started a kicking drill.

Chelsea was right behind me. Since I am much better at kicking than I am at any of the things she sees me doing at school, I was really glad she was going to get a close-up view of me doing it.

I was careful not to look at her after I kicked the bag. I just did it, and then turned and ran to the end of the line as if I were too cool to care. Then, while I was standing there in fighting stance, bouncing up and down, staying loose, she came running back to the end of the line after her kick.

But the only kick I could do on a heavy bag was a roundhouse kick. It got boring doing the same kick over and over again while the higher-ranked students were doing spin kicks and combinations I hadn't learned yet. So after I'd been through the line a couple of times, I started trying to place my kicks higher up on the bag or to kick harder so the bag would wobble more. Before long, each time I hit the bag, it would wobble so hard that Chelsea had to wait for it to stop before she could kick.

"You're going a little overboard, Kyle," Tim warned from where he was watching us and instructing people on how to improve their form. "Use a little less power."

I nodded my head. And I was going to do that. I was going to stay in control and be more careful the next time I kicked. But then Chelsea came running past me so she could get in line, and for just a second our eyes met.

I forgot what I was doing and when I got my next turn at the bag, I kicked it so hard it went right down on its side. And

Chelsea actually laughed when I leaned down to pull it back up.

Mr. Goldman shouted across the dojang and said I had to do ten push-ups, so I lost my place in line ahead of her. But so what? So what? I made Chelsea laugh!

The next morning the book opened up to a new page.

Fighting Fires

As soon as one problem is taken care of, another one pops up. If you let it get you down, you'll be down all the time. And who wants to form a satisfying relationship with someone who isn't cheery? Think of yourself as a fire-fighter and life as a long, long, long series of little brush-fires. The little fires will start to burn, and you will put them out. Most of the time.

Oh, no, I thought as I finished reading the passage. This was definitely a warning. Wasn't it? Didn't it mean there was a new problem coming?

On the way to school, I jumped whenever the bus driver braked or even slowed down for another bus stop. I kept looking for signs that something was wrong in advisory. But the only unusual thing that happened was Melissa's late arrival without a pass. That was her brushfire to fight, not mine.

I started to relax a little after math because we had a pop quiz that I couldn't possibly have done well on. That might have been what *Happy Kid!* was trying to warn me about. Then in art Mr. Ruby told us we'd be handing in all our class work—which, in my case, was not a lot—the next week. If that was what *Happy Kid!* had been tipping me off about, I definitely wished the message had been clearer and come earlier.

By the time I got to social studies, I thought I'd already found my problems for the day. So when I noticed the room was a little quieter than usual, I didn't think much about it. Melissa was whispering excitedly with Chelsea and another girl at the back of the room. Chelsea kept shaking her head no and looked mad, which was exactly how I thought any girl Melissa was hassling ought to look. But instead of wondering what they were whispering about, I imagined the two of them fighting. In my mind, Chelsea took care of Melissa with a few well-placed kicks. Melissa never got close enough to her to land a punch.

Then I got to English.

Melissa was up at Mr. Borden's desk, the way she was always up at the teachers' desks before class. All the other people in the room had silently slipped into their seats and were sitting there as if they were waiting for something to happen.

Melissa said, "Ah, Mr. Borden?" in a low voice that sounded a little worried, though it was hard to tell because I'd never heard her sound worried before. "Did you see the English portion of the State Student Assessment Surveys?"

Mr. Borden finished writing something on a piece of paper

before he answered. "Not until after the tests were given. English teachers aren't allowed to give the English portion of the test to their advisories."

"So you know they gave us a question that we had practiced in class? The 'Are we alone?' essay?"

"Yes."

"And is that okay?"

Mr. Borden shrugged, shook his head, and said, "I don't know. I found the essay question on an old test in a filing cabinet belonging to the head of the English Department." His voice grew a little louder. He wasn't shouting, just making sure Melissa wasn't the only person who could hear him. "We were told we could use them. I certainly didn't cheat, if that's what you're implying."

Melissa's mouth dropped open, and she stepped back as if Mr. Borden had taken a swing at her. "No. I just wanted to know if it was okay that we saw the question before the test."

Mr. Borden looked as if he was a little embarrassed about having accused Melissa of accusing *him* of cheating. Especially since everyone in the class had just heard him do it. He started speaking to all of us, not just Melissa. "Here's the problem: If I start asking questions about whether or not we should have used that essay for practice, this class could end up having to take the English portion of the SSASie over again. That seems like a lot to put so many of you through when no one intended to do anything wrong. I guess the people who make the tests must recycle questions every few years. I happened to pick an old question they were getting ready to recycle. I think it's okay for you to figure you were lucky."

Everyone in the class looked shaken, the way you do when you've just avoided being hit by a car you didn't see coming in the first place. Except for Melissa, who looked as if she'd just found a dead body. Personally, I agreed with Mr. Borden. I felt very, very lucky to have seen that essay question before the day of the test. My essay was going to have to make up for any mistakes I might have made on the rest of the English SSASie. Oh, yes. I was feeling lucky, lucky, lucky.

"What got Melissa going about the SSASies today?" I asked Brad on our way out of class.

"The article on revising the SSASies that I used for current events last Friday," Brad said, looking embarrassed. "She's decided that we got some kind of unfair advantage on the English test because we had a chance to practice writing the essay."

"But it was an accident," I reminded him. "It wasn't the only essay Mr. Borden gave us in September."

"We all told her that when she tried to get us to speak to him with her. Nobody wanted any part of that. But she always wants to do the right thing." Brad sighed.

"Melissa?" I asked in disbelief. "Really?"

"Oh, yeah. I went to grade school with her. I bet she brings it up again. Believe me, she is nuts that way," Brad told me just before we separated outside the cafeteria.

I believed him.

When I got to science class that afternoon, I started wondering if *Happy Kid!* really had been trying to warn me about that math quiz or turning in my art assignments. Those kinds of things happen all the time. They weren't important enough to be brushfires I had to put out.

Melissa, on the other hand, was another story. The SSASies were my ticket to another year with Chelsea. If we had to take the test over again because of Melissa and write another essay on a different topic, what would be my chances of being able to see Chelsea in that special English class for A-kid eighth-graders?

I was sitting at my desk, getting my science notebook out of my backpack when Luke came rushing down the aisle toward me. "I just got invited to go see *Master Lee II* tonight!" he exclaimed, all excited. "Opening night!"

I dropped my notebook on my desk. "I'd forgotten all about it."

"A kid from my social studies class asked me. Do you know him? Phil Rook?"

I shook my head.

"He asked Blake Levine, too. What about him? Do you know him?"

"No."

"Oh. Well, Phil's dad is going to drive us there," Luke said uncomfortably. "It's sort of Phil's . . . thing. I wish you didn't take those accelerated classes so we could hang out with the same people." Then Luke suddenly brightened up. "Are any of your friends from your social studies or English classes going?"

"Maybe," I answered. It was only quarter after one. Maybe some of them were going. Maybe, now that we'd been in class together for more than an entire year, one of them would call me this afternoon and ask me to go see *Master Lee*. Maybe Luke wouldn't have to feel sorry for me because I had no one to see it with. "Maybe I'll see you there," I said.

"Hey, I'll go see ol' Master Lee with you," a voice said from behind us.

People talk about blood running cold because it really happens. I felt my blood chilling in my veins as I heard those words.

"Ah, gee, Jake—" I stammered.

"Tonight is opening night, right? You look it up in the paper and see when the shows are," Jake said. "And I don't want to go to any early kids' show, either. Look for one of the shows around nine."

This was it. *This* was the brushfire I was supposed to put out.

"I'm not sure if I can make it," I said.

"What do you mean? You hoping for a better invitation?" Jake asked. He sounded really nasty, but in his defense, "You hoping for a better invitation?" was a question that would sound nasty coming from almost anybody.

"Not really," I admitted.

"Okay, then. Find the show times and let me know when we're going."

This is not a brushfire, I thought as Mrs. Lynch started handing papers back to us. This is what people mean when they talk about a raging inferno.

CHAPTER 14

☹ 😐 ☺ 😐 ☹ 😐

Fortunately, *Happy Kid!* opened to another new page that afternoon on the bus ride home.

Make the Best of It!

The people who have the easiest time forming satisfying relationships—and lots of them!—are those who make
the best of bad situations. Those sorts of people are fun
and easy to be with. Others are drawn to them.

"Make the Best of It!" would have been a lot more helpful
if I'd actually wanted Jake Rogers drawn to me so I could
form a "satisfying relationship" with him. But I didn't.

Of course, had any of *Happy Kid!*'s advice and warnings
been very helpful? *I* didn't think so.

The phone rang about fifteen minutes after Lauren and I
got home.

"When is your mother picking me up tonight?" Jake asked.

"Oh. I haven't checked the paper yet. We might have to go

another night," I suggested, hoping "another night" would end up being not at all.

"Good thing I went on-line and got the show times. There's one at eight-fifty-five tonight. We'd better get there at eight o'clock. Oh, nah. We'd better get there at seven-forty-five. So be at my house around ten after seven."

"We'll be more than an hour early," I said.

"It's opening weekend. We'll stand in line with everyone else. That's the fun of opening weekend. Gotta go. I've got to make some more calls," he concluded, and hung up before I could say anything else.

"You want to go to the movies with *Jake Rogers*?" Mom asked when I told her I needed her to drive the two of us there.

"Isn't it wonderful?" I said. "I'm going to see *Master Lee II: The Undead* on opening night. I am 'fun and easy to be with.' 'Others are drawn to me.' Like Jake."

"I guess you're going to want a dollar because you read another chapter in *Happy Kid!*" Mom replied.

"And a ride to and from the movies. I'm not getting in a car with one of Jake's parents."

My mother got us to the theater at exactly 7:45. She had just driven away when Jake pointed toward the glass wall at the front of the building and said, "Oh, look! Brian and Kenny are already in line."

If ever there was a bad situation, this was it.

Brian and Kenny were the guys Jake ate lunch with. Brian

164

Coxmore stayed back in third and fifth grades and was now doing his second year of eighth. He wore a goatee and had a driving permit. Kenny Ferris was the only thirteen-year-old I knew who shaved his head.

I guessed I was going to the movies with them. I hoped they wouldn't hurt me.

"Isn't that your sister over there? The one making out with some guy over against the wall?" Jake asked after we'd paid and joined the line of ticket holders.

Sure enough, there were Lauren and Jared, waiting in line to see another movie and carrying on the way they do when they were home on our couch.

"That's her boyfriend," I said.

"He can't do that to her. This is a public place. Let's go beat the crap out of him," Brian suggested.

"Really. She doesn't mind," I said.

"I don't, either," Brian replied. "I just feel like beating the crap out of somebody."

Kenny and Jake laughed. Several people near us shifted a few steps away.

Lauren just happened to look over Jared's shoulder then and saw me. She pushed Jared away and signaled for me to come over. I shook my head. She stamped her foot and signaled again. I shook my head again. Then she looked as if she were going to come over to me.

"I'm going to go beat the crap out of him myself," I told Brian as I took off across the lobby.

"We'd come help, but we don't want to give up our place in line," Kenny shouted.

"I'll go!" Brian offered.

"Don't sweat it," I heard Jake tell him. "Ol' Kyle knows taekwondo."

"You are in so much trouble," Lauren hissed when I was almost near enough to her to carry on a normal conversation. "When Mom and Dad find out who you and Jake met here, you will never be allowed to leave the house again."

"I didn't know Brian and Kenny were going to be here."

"This is what you get for going somewhere with Jake Rogers," Lauren said, sounding more like somebody's mom than somebody's sister who had just been groping with her boyfriend in a theater lobby.

"I'm going—to—to—make the best of this bad situation," I stammered.

"Who are you trying to kid? You have never made the best of a bad situation in your entire life," Lauren objected. "As soon as you find yourself in a bad situation, you go right off the deep end and make it worse. Just how do you, of all people, plan to make the best of this?"

"I don't have a clue," I admitted. "I'm hoping something will come to me."

"Well, good luck. And I am sorry, but Mom is going to have to hear about this," Lauren announced.

"Yeah. Just like she's going to have to hear about the little show the two of you have been putting on for the hundreds of people in this lobby," I said.

"We're dressed. We're standing up. We're not doing anything wrong," Lauren insisted.

"You stop it or the guys I'm with are going to come over here and beat the crap out of Jared. They said so. I don't know if I'll be able to stop them."

"Really?" Lauren asked, sounding interested.

Jared held up his hands. "I won't touch her again until the lights go out in the theater."

"You're not touching me then," Lauren announced. "I want to be able to watch the movie."

Jared looked so disappointed that I had to wonder just what he'd expected to be doing once the lights went out.

"Be careful," Lauren told me as I turned to get back in line.

"You too."

I was heading back through the crowd in the lobby when I saw them.

A-kids. Four of them. Melissa Esposito, Bradley Ryder, a girl who sat over by the windows in English, and . . . Chelsea.

How come I wasn't there? How come I had never been invited to go anywhere with them?

And wasn't Brad standing awfully close to Chelsea? Were they . . . a couple?

I quickly turned so they wouldn't see me. See me there. Without them.

I am seeing *Master Lee II: The Undead* on opening night, I reminded myself. Someday Brad and Chelsea will be "drawn to me" because I made the best of this bad situation. I hope that day will come soon.

I huddled up with Jake, Brian, and Kenny while they talked about some girl in the line Jake thought was hot. I would have loved to see what a girl had to look like for Jake to consider her hot, but she was standing somewhere in front of us and I was trying to keep my back to the front of the line to make sure Chelsea and the others didn't see me. At the same time, I didn't want Jake and his posse to know that I was trying to keep Chelsea and the A-kids from seeing me with them. And what if Luke was here somewhere? What if he saw me and shouted "Hey, Kyle!" from across the lobby? Which normally would be great, but not now, when he'd give me away to Chelsea and the others.

Talk about things not going the way you expect them to, surprises . . . oh, there must have been five or six *Happy Kid!* words of wisdom that would have fit that situation.

"Catfight!" Kenny suddenly said, way too loudly.

I spun around. "Girls fighting? Really? Where?"

"Melissa Esposito is getting ready to pop Chelsea Donahue," Jake explained, pointing up ahead to where Melissa was waving her hands at Chelsea and leaning in toward her while her mouth went a mile a minute. "Go! Go! Go! Go!"

I held my breath. Was Chelsea going to kick Melissa the way I'd imagined that afternoon? No such luck. Chelsea just stood with her arms crossed and looked disgusted while Melissa talked and talked.

I turned my back to them again. "I saw Melissa arguing with Chelsea at school today, too. I think they were fighting about a teacher Melissa thinks cheated or something on one of the SSASies. I don't know what she expects anybody to do about it."

"A teacher cheating? Cool. How?" Jake asked.

"He gave us an essay question for SSASie practice that he found on an old test, and then it ended up being on the real test," I explained.

"So you got a chance to practice writing the essay before the test? That's not fair," Kenny complained. "Not that I wouldn't have done it myself, if I'd had a chance."

"We didn't do it on purpose," I told him.

"I would have."

"We didn't try to cheat," I said, trying to make myself very clear.

"I would have," Kenny said again. He shook his head sadly. "How come I never get teachers who cheat?"

"He wasn't *trying* to cheat! He didn't know it was going to happen."

"Oh, that wasn't cheating then. That was an irregularity," Jake told us.

Kenny and Brian nodded their heads while I said, "A what?"

"I've heard them talking about irregularities in guidance when I'm down there," Jake explained.

"Me too," Kenny said.

"I heard it a couple of years ago when I had that old lady guidance counselor who died," Brian said. "Hey, don't look at me like that. I said she was old. I didn't have anything to do with it."

"How do you get an 'irregularity' with a test?" I asked.

"It's anything other than cheating that can mess up the scores. Like if a student had an unfair advantage—the way you did—or a teacher gave the wrong instructions. I remember because 'irregularity' is another word for 'constipation,' " Jake concluded.

"That's right," Brian said.

"It is," Kenny agreed.

"Is it a big deal?" I wanted to know.

"Constipation?" Brian asked.

"No! This messing up the scores thing," I said.

Jake shrugged. "If I know the people down in the guidance office—and I do—they'll probably just throw out the tests involved and make everyone take them over again."

"Oh, no!" I exclaimed.

"He's right," Brian said while Kenny nodded.

"I don't want to take the test again!"

I looked over my shoulder to see if I could find Melissa. This was just the kind of thing you could expect from her, I thought. She could wreck everything.

But I *am* seeing *Master Lee II* on opening night, I told myself, thinking positively.

"Hey, look. Alldredge is in back of us. I didn't know he was into Master Lee. We can talk about the movie when I'm in his office on Monday," Jake said.

I froze. I couldn't turn away because I didn't want the

A-kids to see me with Jake. But if I stayed where I was, the school principal might see me with him, and Mr. Alldredge already thought I was Jake's "man." I finally crouched down to retie both my shoes a few times, and when I stood up, I was hidden between Jake and Brian and turned so that if Chelsea and Brad or Mr. Alldredge caught a glimpse of me, they wouldn't see more than my profile.

"Is that his wife he's got with him or his mother?" Kenny asked.

"She's not old enough to be his mother. She's kind of porky, though," Brian observed.

"What do you think?" Jake asked me. "Wife or mother?"

I gave Mr. Alldredge a break and said, "Wife."

"She's not over there," Jake complained when he noticed where I was looking. He grabbed me by my shoulders and spun me toward the back of the line. "See Gus? See the woman standing next to Gus?"

"Gus" looked our way as if he'd heard someone calling his name. He ended up staring right at me.

"Wife," I said again as Mr. Alldredge made a face and looked away.

By the time we finally got into the theater, I was thinking that this better be the greatest movie ever made.

We ended up in the very back row, as if I couldn't have seen that coming. Chelsea and Bradley were a third of the way down. Their group had good seats, high up but not in the section where the tough kids liked to hang out. No, that's where I was.

Mr. Alldredge got stuck two rows ahead of us. The woman he was with, who really was pretty chunky, had taken so much time deciding where she wanted to sit that a lot of the good rows had filled up.

"You know, I've heard that Master Lee dies at the end of this thing," Jake said.

"Bummer," Kenny replied.

"What did you tell me that for?" Brian complained. "What's the point of seeing the movie now?"

"Oh, come on. They're not going to kill off Master Lee. They need him so they can make a third movie," I told him.

"He's right. I was lying," Jake admitted.

"You're ugly. I'm not lying," Brian said.

The lights went out, and I sat up a little straighter since I figured I was safe in the dark.

The movie *was* good. And I *was* seeing it on opening night. I would be able to talk to people about it on Monday. They didn't have to know how I came to see it. I had not gone off the deep end over this bad situation, I had made the best of it the way *Happy Kid!* said I should.

I had just noticed one of Master Lee's zombies doing some moves I'd seen some of the higher-ranked students doing at the dojang when I suddenly noticed an odor settling around us like a cloud. People around us were wiggling in their seats and trying to lean away. There were mutters and groans. Brian and Kenny started to laugh and poke at Jake.

"Can you believe it?" he said in a loud whisper that carried so far that people five rows ahead of us were turning around and scowling. "Gus cut one."

I just froze in my seat. Mr. Alldredge turned around to look at us. He looked far, far madder than he had when he'd thought I had a weapon on a school bus.

I didn't think he knew how to make the best of his bad situation.

CHAPTER 15

☹ 😐 🙂 😐 ☹ 😐

"Why did we go to an early show?" Luke wailed while we stood in line in the cafeteria on Monday. "Why couldn't I have been there?"

"Oh, there were about ten minutes when you wouldn't have wanted to be there," I assured him. "No one wanted to be there. Jake doesn't even try to control himself."

"I think he can fart at will. You have to admit, that's impressive," Luke said.

"What impresses me is that he never, ever gets embarrassed. He's not like normal people," I pointed out. "Maybe he's not really human."

We'd paid for our lunches and were walking to our table.

"So Mr. Alldredge didn't think you accused him of farting, did he?" Luke asked.

"Nah. Jake called him Gus. No one does that except for him. I'm just going to get blamed for being with Jake."

Luke started to laugh hysterically. He just managed to say, "Maybe Mr. Alldredge thought you were the one who farted."

Yeah, that was real funny. I wasn't too concerned about Mr. Alldredge thinking I'd farted in a movie theater, though, because I was so busy worrying about what I'd read over the weekend.

The title of the latest new chapter in *Happy Kid!* was "Help!"

I saw that and thought, Good. This message will help me out in some way.

Hardly.

Help!

You'll never form satisfying relationships if you only think of yourself and just take care of your own workload. Somebody needs your help. It wouldn't kill you to lend a hand. Working together with others is working *together with others.*

Call me negative, but somehow I just knew it wasn't going to be someone good like, say, Chelsea who needed my help.

Two more days passed. Wednesday came and no one had needed my help. But I knew someone would because *Happy Kid!* was still opening to that same page. I made it safely through the first three periods of the day. Then, just after I left social studies, I felt someone grabbing at my arm.

"I called your name two or three times," Melissa complained. "I need you to help me with something."

"If you're looking for my scene for Borden's Playhouse, I finished it over the weekend," I said.

"Oh. You didn't think to make copies for the other people on the creative team, did you?"

"Yes, I did."

"That's great. That's really great."

I'd helped her! That was all I had to do. What a relief.

Then Melissa blurted, "Will you also go to Mr. Alldredge's office with me to tell him about that essay question we shouldn't have seen before we took the SSASies?"

"Are you out of your mind?" I gasped.

"I'll make the appointment and do all the talking," Melissa said.

"No, I won't go with you!"

"Why not?" Melissa demanded.

"Because I don't want to. Nobody did anything wrong. Intentionally. It was an accident. It was an irregularity."

"That's right!" Melissa exclaimed. "I read some newspaper articles about school testing, and they used that exact word! You're the only person who knew that."

"Jake Rogers knows it. So do Brian Coxmore and Kenny Ferris."

"You're kidding! How did *they* know that when none of the kids in any of my accelerated classes knew it?"

"I'm in a couple of your accelerated classes, remember? And I knew it," I pointed out.

"So you understand why it's wrong to just pretend it didn't happen? You understand why it should be reported so we can take the test again and get correct scores?"

"What do you mean 'we'? You wrote on the other essay

topic, remember? You wouldn't even be involved with this. You just want to make everyone else do extra work," I said.

"That's not the way the system works," Melissa explained, as if she were some kind of expert on the subject. "Mr. Borden explained it in class that day. If there's an irregularity in giving the test to a *group*, the whole *group* has to be retested. I had the same advantage everyone else did. Who knows what I would have done on test day if I hadn't already seen one of the questions?"

My mouth dropped open for a moment and then I said, "You wrote an essay on the *second* question because Mr. Borden told you the answer you wrote to the first one for class would have received a low score. I'll say you had an advantage."

Melissa looked as if she was going to burst into flame right in front of me.

"That's not why I used the second question! I never even thought of that! Never! I was just trying to behave like a decent person. Which question did you choose, as if I have to ask. And why did you choose it? Again, as if I have to ask."

This argument wasn't going to lead to anything good for me. Besides, if Melissa didn't calm down, I was afraid people would start to stare at us.

"Why do you even want me to go with you, anyway?" I asked. "You hardly ever speak to me except to complain about something. I would have thought you'd have asked one of the A-kids."

"The 'A-kids'?" Melissa repeated. I'd definitely distracted her from her rant.

"You know. The kids who are in all those accelerated classes you take."

Melissa laughed. "That's what you call them? That's good. That fits."

"You're one of them!" I exclaimed.

"So are you. You're in two accelerated classes. Remember?"

Oh, if she only knew how I'd gotten into those classes. I very carefully didn't tell her.

"Ask someone else to go with you," I said instead.

"I already have," she admitted.

"Who?"

"Everybody in our English class. They all said no."

"All of them? Brad? Chelsea?" I asked.

"That's what I just told you," Melissa snapped. "They all said no."

"Then you shouldn't be surprised to hear that I'm saying no, too." If Chelsea said no, I sure wasn't going to say yes.

"Why won't you go?" Melissa asked.

"For the same reason they wouldn't go," I answered.

"Which is?"

We were right outside our English class, which was not the greatest place to be talking about this. We also were running out of time.

"Whatever they said," I answered vaguely.

"You think Mr. Borden's a real nice guy and don't want to get him in trouble?"

178

"Oh, come on! They said that?" She had to be making that up.

" 'A-kids' like their teachers," Melissa pointed out.

"I've noticed that," I admitted.

Any fool could see that Melissa was the somebody who needed the help *Happy Kid!* was talking about. I didn't care. When I thought of the phrase "working together with others," Melissa was not the first "other" who came to my mind. She didn't even make the Top Ten.

"Class is going to start," I told her and walked past her into our classroom.

I was able to avoid Melissa most of Thursday morning because I had an orthodontist appointment and got to school just as third period was starting. I latched on to Brad on the way to English so she wouldn't be on me during the walk between classes. One of the other guy A-kids rushed up to join us.

"I don't want to be alone in the hall." He laughed. "I'm afraid Melissa might get me."

"Me too," I said.

"She asked *you* to go see Mr. Alldredge with her?" Brad asked.

I could have gotten all upset because he sounded surprised that Melissa would ask for my help with a job no one else wanted. Then I decided to take the attitude of hey, two A-kids are walking and talking with me. What more do I want?

"Yeah, I couldn't believe she was asking me, either. But once all you guys said no, I was all that was left," I said. "How long do you think it will be before she gives up?"

"She'll go by herself before she gives up," Brad answered. "When we were in fifth grade, she was the only kid in her classroom who would eat lunch at the special-ed kids' table. She didn't do it all the time, and there weren't any kids there she was friends with. She said it was the right thing to do."

"Let me guess," I said. "She went around bugging everyone else, trying to make them do it, too?"

Brad laughed. "She got me to do it once. The really funny part is the special-ed kids didn't like her. They wanted her to leave them alone."

"You know what the funny part about this testing business is?" the other A-kid asked. "Melissa is right. We did have an unfair advantage because we had a chance to practice that essay question. It's just . . . I don't know how to put it, but . . ."

"Sometimes you can be *too* right?" Brad suggested.

The other boy laughed and said to me, "We've known her since first grade." He turned back to Brad and asked, "Do you remember back in second grade how she used to run tattling to the teacher all the time when other kids did things they weren't supposed to?"

"Oh, yeah," Brad recalled. "She wasn't even trying to get anyone in trouble. She just thought she was doing the right thing. She just didn't understand that—"

"—sometimes you can be *too* right!" the other A-kid recited along with him.

For a fraction of a second, a really short one, I almost felt sorry for Melissa because she couldn't quite figure out how to get along in life the way all the other A-kids had. But it passed quickly because the three of us there in the hallway were laughing, and then a couple of other A-kids joined us. By the time I entered our English classroom, I was surrounded by people and not thinking about Melissa at all.

I kept checking *Happy Kid!* hoping it would open to a new message. No such luck. At taekwondo on Thursday night I got confused while I was doing my form, and Mr. Goldman sent me to the back of the dojang to practice on my own for a while. He said I still wasn't controlling myself. (I *may* have stopped and stamped my foot or something when I realized that another white belt was going one way while I was going the other.) I thought for sure after that there'd be a new message from *Happy Kid!* It seemed like a good time for it to pop open to a page on how everyone loves people who are humble and listen to their teachers or how it takes patience to form satisfying relationships.

But no. All I found was "Help!"

Melissa was waiting at my locker Friday morning.

"I have an appointment with Mr. Alldredge at three o'clock on Monday afternoon," Melissa began.

"Good for you!"

"It would be really helpful if you came with me," she said. "I should have someone else there who knows that we had a chance to practice the essay."

"No, it would not be helpful to have me there," I said.

Instead of arguing with me, she reached into her backpack, which she had propped on the floor next to her feet, and pulled out some papers. "I want you to read these. They're the newspaper articles I found on the Internet."

"Thank you, anyway, but I already have an article for current events."

"These articles are all about other teachers and schools that made mistakes with their standardized tests. It was a mistake for us to practice that essay before the SSASies," Melissa insisted.

"That's right. It was a *mistake*. Mistakes happen. Get over it. Get over yourself," I added for good measure. "You're being really negative about this, by the way. You're only seeing the worst in this situation."

"What would be a positive way of looking at this situation?" Melissa asked.

"I have a good shot at getting into the ninth-grade English class offered for eighth-graders because I accidentally practiced that essay is a positive way of looking at it. I want to be in that class next year. And since no one really cheated, I don't see any problem with this situation. Just the opposite. It's all good."

"So you would have to take the test again. Big deal! So what?" Melissa exclaimed.

"That's easy for you to say. You're an A-kid," I reminded her.

"You are, too."

"Yeah, well," I said uncomfortably, since I knew that wasn't exactly true, "you do not want *me* to go see Mr. Alldredge with you. I am the guy who sat in Alldredge's office with a state trooper last year. I am the guy he thought was going to use a screwdriver as some kind of weapon of mass destruction."

If she were a really nice person instead of Melissa, she would have said, "Oh, that's all in your head! No one ever thought that!" Instead she said, "I think that could work for us. We'd be a student leader and a—whatever you are—banding together for a common cause. That would make our argument a lot stronger."

"Mr. Alldredge also thinks I'm part of Jake Rogers's posse. Will that work for us?"

Melissa made a face. "Why do you insist on hanging around with Jake?"

"He hangs around with me."

"Well, it can't be helped."

"I'm not going with you! You're just going to make trouble," I told her. "You'll have to do it by yourself."

"Why is it so wrong of me to want to do the right thing?" Melissa asked.

"If you're so sure you're right, why don't you go by yourself?"

"I don't want to go there alone. I've never done anything like this before," Melissa explained.

"No? I heard you used to tattle when you were in second grade," I said.

Melissa gasped. "I was seven years old! I didn't know any better. Why won't people forget about that? Who told you, anyway?"

"It doesn't matter. I shouldn't have said anything."

She grabbed my arm as I started to go into advisory and made me stay out in the hall with her.

"Do you remember that *Happy Kid!* book?"

"What about it?" I asked suspiciously.

"If you don't come with me on Monday, I'm going to tell everyone you were reading it. Everyone will know you're a loser who needs a self-help book."

I pulled my arm away from her. "Go ahead. I've had people talk about me before."

I hoped I looked cool as I walked across the classroom to my desk because inside I was screaming, Everyone is going to know!

"Kyle's got himself a woman," Jake said before he even had his flabby self settled on his stool in the art room.

"Who?" I asked. I didn't actually "have" Chelsea, so I didn't think he could be talking about her.

"I saw you walking with Melissa Esposito in the hall this morning. Did you get her to rub her great big chest all over you?" Jake asked.

"People who really know Melissa hardly notice her great big chest because of her great big mouth," I answered.

"Oh. Did she rub *that* all over you?"

"She's trying to get me to go with her to see Mr. Alldredge," I said between gritted teeth.

"Tell her that if she rubs her great big chest all over you, you'll do it," Jake suggested.

"She wants us to tell Mr. Alldredge about that essay question we practiced before we answered it on the English SSASie," I told him.

"Why?" Jake asked.

"Because it's the 'right' thing to do. She's very big on doing the 'right' thing."

Jake looked thoughtful and said, "Hmmm. The 'right' thing. You'll have to explain that to me. I don't think I've ever heard of that before."

Luke had stopped working on his paper and was looking at me. "You practiced answering one of the essay questions that we had on the SSASies? That's not fair."

"It was an accident," I explained for what seemed like the millionth time. "Our English teacher found old SSASies in a filing cabinet, took essay questions off of them, and gave the questions to us for writing assignments. Nobody knew one was going to be on this year's test."

"It's still not fair," Luke objected. "You guys are going to get better scores than everyone else."

"They would have gotten better scores than the rest of us, anyway," Jake said. "One essay won't change anything. They're just going to beat us by more, that's all."

"It's not a contest," I objected. "We just don't want to have to take the test over again. And if Melissa tells Mr. Alldredge about it, we'll have to."

"You *should* have to take the test over again. You're cheating because you want to look smarter than the rest of us. You guys are already the smart kids," Luke said angrily.

"What's going on over there?" Mr. Ruby called from the back of the room.

"We've got a fight going. Don't worry about it. I'll break them up," Jake shouted over his shoulder. Then he turned back to us. "Best two out of three rounds? And, yes, you may bite and punch below the belt."

"Luke," I whispered because a lot of people were turning to look at us. "I've never wanted to look smarter than you. I couldn't, even if I wanted to. And I'm not cheating. I told you how it happened. The whole thing was an accident. No one did anything wrong."

"Maybe what happened with the test was an accident, but what you're doing now isn't an accident. You're intentionally doing something wrong because you don't want to fix what happened the day of the test," Luke told me. "*Now* you're cheating."

I opened my mouth to tell Luke that he didn't understand, that the tests didn't mean anything for us because they were a test to see if the schools were doing well. But they did mean something to me. I was hoping they would get me into those special courses.

Jake sighed dramatically and shook his head. "I'd go tell Gus about this whole thing, myself, because it would be so much fun to see him have to take care of a screwup that I didn't have anything to do with. But I don't think I can bring myself to snitch. Even on a teacher. A guy's gotta have some standards, you know."

Cheating? Snitching? There was no way I could get out of this mess without doing something that somebody wouldn't like.

Why didn't *Happy Kid!* do something about this? Why didn't it help *me*?

CHAPTER 16

☹ 😐 ☺ 🙂 ☹ 😐

I had to force myself down the hall to social studies, where I was greeted by a cluster of A-kids who had heard about Melissa grabbing me in the hall.

"Better you than me," one of them said, laughing.

"I can't believe she won't give this up," one of the girls complained. "What is she thinking?"

"She hasn't bothered anyone else since Wednesday. She's determined to get you now," the first speaker told me.

"I'm her last chance," I agreed.

Brad slapped me on the back. "Don't give in. Like I said before, if she can't get anyone to go with her, I'm betting she'll go by herself. Once she does that, she'll leave the rest of us alone."

Us. Which included me.

"She has an appointment with Mr. Alldredge on Monday afternoon," I told them. "So I only have to put up with her for about three and a half more days. And two of those are Saturday and Sunday. I should be able to do that."

"She made an appointment?" a girl gasped. "Shouldn't somebody try to stop her?"

"Any volunteers?" Brad asked.

Oh, wow. What if this is it? I thought. What if I'm supposed to help the A-kids stop Melissa?

"The next time she tries to convince *me* to go with her, I could try to convince *her* not to go at all," I offered.

The others seemed very satisfied with that suggestion. They didn't have to do anything, and I had only promised "to try."

Helping the A-kids was going to be easy.

I was part of a group that walked together to English class. And in English class my creative team finally performed "Scenes from *The Odyssey.*" The five of us were all together at the front of the room, waiting our turns to speak, helping each other find our parts on the pages. It was like being at taekwondo because after a while I forgot Luke was mad at me and Melissa was trying to get me to do something no one else wanted to do. I got totally into playing my parts. So they weren't great parts. I played one of Odysseus's men who are turned into pigs by Circe and then one of the men who wanted to force Odysseus's wife to marry him and let him take over Odysseus's kingdom. But everyone was laughing between scenes, even Melissa. There was applause and shouts of "Again! Again!" after the guy playing Odysseus got me with his imaginary sword and I spun around and died.

When we finished the scene I'd written, in which I made Odysseus stupid and greedy and showed him stealing from the Cyclops and picking on him, Mr. Borden said I'd done some original work.

And he made it sound as if it was a good thing. He said it right out loud in front of everybody. In front of Chelsea.

The A-kids were right. Mr. Borden was a real nice guy. Well, maybe he wasn't a real nice guy. But he was okay. He was definitely okay.

I think Chelsea was impressed, because after class when a group of us gathered out in the hall for a few minutes to talk about Melissa, she and a couple of her girlfriends joined us. She got there just in time to hear someone say, "If Melissa tells Mr. Alldredge about it, we'll have to take the test over. It's not fair. Why should we be punished like that when we've done nothing wrong?"

Chelsea nodded her head in agreement, and so did I. A couple of other kids said things, and Chelsea and I nodded again, agreeing with them and agreeing with each other. It was almost as if I was having a conversation with her. Except that someone else was doing all the talking.

I was going to have to walk right past Chelsea to get to the cafeteria, anyway, so I started slowly moving in that direction along with all the other kids who were walking past us in the hallway. I was hoping I could stop and stand beside her for a little while. I was almost next to her when I heard someone come up behind me and stop.

"You on your way to the cafeteria?" Luke asked.

"I, uh, need a couple of minutes," I said.

"I'll wait," Luke offered.

He sounded particularly nice and even kind of serious, which made me think he was feeling bad because we'd been arguing in art class. I wanted to go with him, but I wanted to stay with the A-kids, too. And they had stopped talking and were waiting for me.

"I'll meet you later, okay?" I said to him.

Luke noticed everyone watching and took the hint. His face fell, and he muttered, "Yeah. Right."

He started to move again, and then one of the A-kids said, "Sure, it would make a difference if a mistake had been made with some of the other kids' SSASies. But we're going to get good scores on the test no matter what essay question they use. So what's the point of making us do it over?"

Luke heard every word. He stopped, turned around, and stared right at me for a moment. He had this look on his face as if he'd just been slapped.

I should have at least said "see ya later" or something to Chelsea, but I didn't think of it because I was in such a rush to get to Luke so I could try to fix things.

"I'm ready for lunch," I said as I caught up with him.

"It's okay. You can meet me later."

"I'm ready to meet you now," I told him.

"I didn't mean to interrupt you when you were with . . . those guys."

"Luke? Does it bother you that I'm in accelerated classes?" I asked.

"Of course it does! We stopped doing things together after you got into classes with those better kids."

"It wasn't because I was with them. It was because you and I weren't in any classes together last year the way we are this year. We never saw each other," I explained.

"So what? You could have asked me to do things with you, but you didn't," he said.

"*You* could have asked *me,* but you didn't," I reminded him. "And those kids aren't 'better.' They're just smart. That's not the same as better."

"If they're not better, then how come they don't have to follow the same rules the rest of us do? How come it's okay for them to cheat so they don't have to take that test over again?"

"It's not cheating!" I yelled in the middle of the hallway.

"If you and your friends don't see what's wrong about not reporting this 'mistake,' then you aren't really all that smart," Luke said just before he marched ahead of me into the cafeteria.

"We are so!" I shouted after him and took off in another direction.

Then I was stuck. It was lunchtime, and I was supposed to be in the cafeteria, too. But what was I supposed to do? Sit with Luke? We were fighting. My only other option was sitting at Jake's table.

I headed off for a boys' room. I leaned against a wall and slid down until I was sitting on my backpack.

This is nice, I thought as I sat with my back against the cool tile wall. Schools should have rooms like this where people can go when they want to be by themselves for a while.

Rooms where they don't have to sit on the floor between a trash can and a urinal, though.

The door out to the hall suddenly opened, and I heard someone's shoes hitting the floor as he walked in. I didn't look up until he spoke.

"What are you doing here?" Mr. Kowsz asked.

"I totally lost control of myself a little while ago."

"Oh? Did you kick anybody?"

"No!"

"Break anything? Shout obscenities at a teacher?"

"No. I yelled at somebody in the hall."

"It's probably nothing that can't be fixed, then."

"I don't know how to fix it."

Mr. Kowsz hesitated and then asked, "Does this have anything to do with a girl? If it's a girl, you'll get over it. With some girls it takes longer than others. For instance, if the girl was your wife for twenty-five years who left you—"

"No, no, no. It's not about a girl," I said before Mr. Kowsz could say any more.

"Where are you supposed to be now?" he asked.

"This is my lunch period. I just want to stay here."

"You can't. I'll give you a pass so you can go to my classroom until your next class starts. I won't be there," Mr. Kowsz added, as if that would make staying in his classroom more desirable. Which it did. "I'm on my lunch break. I've got to hit all the bathrooms and then get my coffee down at the teachers' lounge. You'll be by yourself in my room except for a couple of kids who play cards there at this time of day."

I stood up. "You let kids play cards in your room?"

Mr. Kowsz shrugged. "Some people really don't like being in the cafeteria. If they're kids I know and I'm sure they won't play with any of my equipment, I'll let them use my room for something quiet like cards or chess. Don't tell anybody. There aren't that many kids I trust to leave alone in there."

He trusted me.

"Listen," I said as we walked along the hallway together. "How bad would it be if a teacher accidentally gave a class an essay assignment to help them practice for the SSASies and the essay later ended up being on the actual test?"

Mr. Kowsz's head swiveled toward me, and he had that look he gets when he thinks he smells smoke or hears someone out in the hallway during class time.

He never finished his tour of the boys' rooms or got his coffee in the teachers' lounge. Instead, he stayed in his classroom with me for the rest of the period, which was how long it took for me to tell him the whole story.

It seemed pretty clear to me that Luke thought I ought to help Melissa report the SSASie irregularity. Melissa definitely thought I ought to help report the SSASie irregularity. I was pretty sure Mr. Kowsz thought so, too, because he kept talking about how taekwondo students have some kind of code about right and wrong and helping others in need (another detail nobody mentioned before I started taking classes). Even Jake agreed with them since he said the only thing keeping him from reporting the whole screw-up was his refusal to snitch on other people.

Which I was afraid meant that his standards were better than mine, because the only thing that was keeping *me* from reporting the irregularity was my hope that the essay mistake would mean a higher SSASie test score for me and a chance to stay with Chelsea in eighth grade. To be truthful, it wasn't the only thing that was keeping me from agreeing to help Melissa. *Not* helping her was giving me an in with the A-kids that I had never had before.

I was willing to ignore . . . an irregularity . . . for a girl and popularity. A girl who had never even spoken to me. Popularity with kids who didn't even know my old friends like Luke. Yes, I was well on my way to becoming a worse human being then Jake Rogers.

On top of everything else, there was no doubt what *Happy Kid!* was telling me to do. That "Somebody needs your help" message just wouldn't go away. There was no beating the book. I decided I might as well give in.

Melissa's appointment with Mr. Alldredge was after school on Monday, though, so I was going to need a ride home. Sunday night, while both Nana and Jared were at the house, I decided I'd better start looking for one.

When we were clearing the table after dinner and Nana was talking about leaving, I said, "Oh, can one of you guys give me a ride home from school tomorrow? I have to stay late."

Dad just said, "What time? I have a meeting around two."

Mom nearly dropped a glass and asked, "Why? Why do you have to stay late?"

"I have to help Melissa Esposito with something."

"Really? Help her with what?" Mom asked, sounding as if she'd just heard I'd made honor roll or won a scholarship somewhere.

"It's something to do with our English class. We have to go see Mr. Alldredge about it tomorrow. We have an appointment," I explained.

"*Wonderful*. You've never stayed after school to work on something before. What's the project?" Mom wanted to know. "Come on. Tell us about it."

This was going to be harder than I'd thought. My plan had a flaw, the flaw being that I never expected my mother to get so excited. I didn't want her making a big deal out of going to see Mr. Alldredge. I was already making as big a deal out of it as I could stand.

"Melissa knows more about it than I do," I explained. "She's going to do all the talking."

"I wish you had called me at work Friday afternoon and told me about this. I could have shifted one or two of Monday's appointments then. But it's way too late now. Bobby? Is there anything you can do?" Mom asked my father.

"I'll have to wait until after I get to work tomorrow morning to find out," Dad said.

"Maggie, I hate to ask you," Mom said, turning to Nana.

"Well," Nana said as she pulled on her coat, "I have to get home. Walk me out to my car, Kyle, and we'll talk about it."

Then Nana grabbed me by the ear and dragged me out of the living room with her.

"What's up?" she asked when we got as far as the garage and no one else could hear us.

"Nothing. I'm not in trouble or anything. Really! I just have to do something with this girl, Melissa. She likes to do those 'let's make our school a better place' kinds of projects. We're going to talk to Mr. Alldredge about one of those."

"She may like to do those kinds of projects, but since when do you have anything to do with them? No one in our family has done anything like that since my mother had to help with an Easter egg hunt sponsored by the Future Homemakers of America at her high school. Remind me to tell you how *that* turned out someday. I repeat: What's up?"

The government ought to put my grandmother to work questioning suspected terrorists. She could get anything out of anybody. I ended up telling her everything. Though I did leave out the part about not wanting to take the test over so I'd get a higher score and be with Chelsea next year. And I said absolutely nothing about *Happy Kid!* I like to think my grandmother would believe me when I said I had a book that provided advice and warnings to whoever held it, but I wasn't certain enough to take a chance.

When I finished, Nana shrugged and said, "This shouldn't be your problem. This should be the teacher's problem. He's making it your problem by not reporting the mistake himself. If you tell the principal, it will become *the principal's* problem, and you can be done with it."

"That's exactly what Mr. Kowsz said when I told him about this!" I exclaimed.

"Really?"

"Yeah. So, now that you know the whole thing, will you give me a ride home tomorrow?" I asked.

"What time?"

"I'm not sure," I said. "Sometime after three o'clock. If you come to get me and I'm not ready, why don't you go find Mr. Kowsz's classroom and look at those things he wanted to show you. What were they?"

"Lamp bases," Nana answered immediately. "He makes them out of metal and wood. Are you sure you don't mind if I go see him? You're not just saying this to get me to come pick you up, are you?"

"Yeah, I am," I admitted. "But I don't mind if you go see him. I'm not going to be at Trotts forever. Once I'm gone, if you want to go out with a guy who spends his lunch hours going through the boys' rooms hunting for juvenile delinquents, it's no skin off my back."

"Oh, you make him sound *so* attractive."

"If you do go see him tomorrow, ask him where Mr. Goldman gets the small paddle-shaped targets we use in taekwondo class. I want one for Christmas."

Nana kissed me good-bye. I shut the door after she left and thought, Oh, no. I'm really doing this.

I ran upstairs to my room. Maybe I'd find a new message in *Happy Kid!* And it would be really nice if it were a message that would help with what I had to do the next day.

But no, I let the book open up, and all I got was the same old thing. "Help."

Why didn't it change? Was it going to wait until after we went to the principal's office?

I thought of one more thing I could try to make a new page turn up. I went downstairs to get the phone book. There were five Espositos listed in our town. Of course, Melissa's number was the fifth one I tried.

"Melissa!" a little girl shouted at the other end of the line when I told her who I was looking for. "A boy wants to talk to you! A boy is calling for Melissa! Mom! There's a boy on the phone for Mel!"

Her family called her Mel?

"Hello?" Melissa said, sounding all eager and happy.

"Ah . . . Melissa, it's Kyle."

"Oh."

"I'm calling to tell you that I'll go with you to see Mr. Alldredge tomorrow. Unless . . . you found someone else? Did you?" I asked.

"No. I haven't even been trying. It was hopeless."

"Well, I'll go with you. But you have to do all the talking the way you said you would."

"Fine," Melissa agreed. "I want to do that, anyway."

"And once Mr. Alldredge knows about it, I'm done. If he says we should just figure we were lucky the way Mr. Borden did, then we were lucky."

"Do you think he'll say that?" Melissa asked, sounding worried.

"I don't care what he says. It doesn't matter to me. All that matters is that I go and get this over with."

"That's not a very good attitude," Melissa complained.

"I wouldn't be fussy if I were you! I'm going. What more do you want?"

"Okay. Okay. You don't have to yell."

I said good-bye and hung up as fast as I could. Then I went back upstairs and picked up *Happy Kid!*

All right, book, I said, but not out loud because I'm not actually crazy. I arranged for a ride home, *and* I told Melissa I would go with her. So there's no reason for you to tell me the same old thing. Tell me something I don't know.

Then I let the covers of the book fall apart, and the pages just dropped away from each other. I looked down at a new page.

Be Careful Not to Blame Others

Many people get very touchy if they think they're being accused of something. Anything. If someone thinks he's being blamed for even an accident, he can become a bitter, angry enemy. You'll have a very hard time forming a satisfying relationship with him after that. Watch your step.

"Watch your step." Oh, yes. That was just what I wanted to hear.

CHAPTER 17

☹ 😐 ☺ 😐 ☹ 😐

That night I had a dream about Mr. Borden chasing me up and down the halls of the school. He was waving a screwdriver the size of a broomstick.

As soon as I got to advisory that morning, Melissa started giving orders.

"We really need to plan what we're going to do at our meeting with Mr. Alldredge. Look for me before social studies, and we'll walk together to class."

"The plan is made, Melissa. You said you'd do all the talking," I reminded her.

"I will, I will. I just want you to hear what I'm going to say."

"I don't care what you say so long as you watch your step."

"I think I know how to be careful and sensitive," Melissa retorted, as if I'd accused her of something. "I'll see you before third period."

I thought there was a very real possibility that we were doomed.

"There is something going on between you and Melissa Esposito, isn't there?" Jake asked during art class. We were standing in line by the cupboard where we kept the projects we were working on, so everyone around us could hear.

"Oh, please," I replied.

"I saw you in the hall with her this morning," he said.

"Do you watch everything I do?" I asked, trying not to look up to see who was listening.

"Always. Last week you picked something up off the floor in the cafeteria and ate it."

I didn't think it was worth making the effort to deny that. I did wish I could ask Luke if he'd heard anyone talking about Melissa and me being a couple, though. But after he picked up his project, he took his stool and placed it as far away from me at our table as he could. Not only was he not speaking to me, he wasn't even looking at me.

Once Jake and I were back at our table, I said, "Melissa and I are hanging around together because . . . we're working on something," so Luke would hear me.

He did. He knew what I was talking about right away. He really should be an A-kid. After he'd pulled his stool closer to me, I whispered, "We're going to see Mr. Alldredge this afternoon—about that essay."

"Oh, Kyle, man . . . do you think Mr. Borden will be fired?" Luke whispered back.

"No one said anything about being fired!"

"Kyle!" Mr. Ruby called. "That was way too loud! Do you want to go down to the principal's office?"

"No!" Luke and I shouted together.

"Why would he get fired?" I asked Luke in a lower voice.

"He did screw up and give you guys the wrong essay question for practice."

"But we know it was an accident. We're not *blaming* him for doing something wrong. Why are you bringing this up now? You said I should try to fix what happened," I reminded him.

"Well, sure, but it's going to be so hard to do that."

And he didn't think of that before?

Jake leaned across the table toward us. "What's going on?" he asked.

"Kyle is going to tell Mr. Alldredge about that essay his teacher showed him before the SSASies," Luke explained.

"*I'm* not telling him. Melissa is. I'm just going with her. I'm just going to be there in the room. Not saying anything," I insisted.

"So what did Melissa have to do to get you to go?" Jake asked.

"She had to be right, Jake."

"Kyle, wow, you're just like one of Master Lee's warriors," Luke said.

"One of the *zombies*?"

"Well, yeah, they were dead," Luke admitted, "but they were still cool."

"Tell Melissa that if ol' Gus gives her any trouble when you guys are visiting him, she can just mention my name," Jake told me.

"Thanks, Jake. I think she'll be really pleased to hear that."

She wasn't.

"How can you be friends with him?" she demanded on our way to social studies.

"I'm not. He just always seems to be where I am. By the way, you probably should know that a little over a week ago, Jake and I were in the same movie theater with Mr. Alldredge. Jake farted and blamed it on him."

"Why are you telling me that disgusting story?"

"Because I was sitting next to Jake when it happened, and Mr. Alldredge turned around and saw me there. I don't know that it will matter today, but—"

Melissa stopped dead in the hall. "So Mr. Alldredge really *does* think you're part of Jake's posse?"

"I told you so."

Melissa looked as if someone had punched her in the stomach. "Oh, no, oh, no, oh, no," she kept saying while her eyes kind of bulged out of her head.

"You still want me to go with you?" I asked.

"I'll let you know," she gasped, and she hurried off.

When I walked into social studies, Brad asked, "What's up?"

That could have meant anything. I decided it meant, "Are you going to the principal's office with Melissa this afternoon?" because that was all I could think about. So I just said, "Yes."

"Yes?" Brad repeated.

"I'm going to the principal's office with Melissa this afternoon."

I had been sure he would be shocked or mad or disappointed. But he just nodded and said, "I know how it is. Once or twice last week I almost broke and told her *I'd* go."

"You still can," I offered eagerly. "Melissa's not that happy with me right now."

"That's okay." Brad grinned. "I've been to the principal's office before."

"Me, too. You may have heard about it? A cop was there?"

"Oh, yeah. That sounds familiar," he admitted.

"And why did you have to go?" I asked.

"I was one of the Citizens of the Month in February, and we all went to Mr. Alldredge's office to have lunch with him," Brad said, sounding just a little bit embarrassed.

I thought it would be something like that.

"We're still on for this afternoon," Melissa told me after English. "I'll meet you at your locker right after school."

She looked a little jumpy and pale. The sight of her just filled me with confidence.

It's funny the way time both drags and goes by too fast when you're waiting to do something you really don't want to do. It seemed to take forever for the school day to end, but then, way too soon, there I was standing next to my locker with Melissa.

"Remember, I'm going to do all the talking," she said as we started to walk toward the office.

"That's always been the plan," I reminded her.

"I'm going to do all the talking."

"Yes, Melissa."

"I've been thinking about this for days. I've planned what I'm going to say, so I'll do all the talking."

"Okay," I said, noticing that we seemed to have slowed down.

"Teachers always like me. Don't teachers always like me?" Melissa asked me.

"I guess. I've only known you a year and a half," I told her.

"Teachers always like me, so I should do all the talking."

"Melissa, you're freaking out," I said.

"I am not. Why should I freak out?"

"Your voice is shaking, Mel. Why are you putting yourself through this? Mr. Borden is the one who should be telling Mr. Alldredge about what happened. It hardly has anything to do with us."

"What if everybody said that?" Melissa asked me. "What if everybody said, 'I'm not going to do this thing that somebody needs to do because it's too difficult, or I'm scared, or it hardly has anything to do with me'?"

"According to those articles you keep bringing to current events, that's pretty much what everyone *does* say."

"Should we be that way just because everyone else is?" Melissa asked.

I could have said, "That would be fine with me," but I

didn't want to sound as if I wasn't as good a person as Melissa was. So instead I said, "Let's get this over with. Someone is coming to get me in fifteen or twenty minutes, and she doesn't like to wait."

We had to sit out with the secretaries for a couple of minutes because Mr. Alldredge was on the phone. When he was done he came to the door and said, "Come in, Melissa! Glad to see you! Oh. Kyle. Did one of your teachers send you down here? The detention room is right down the hall—"

"He's with me, Mr. Alldredge," Melissa said.

I had never had detention. Not once. But just as soon as Mr. Alldredge saw me, that's what he thought I was there for.

Talk about thinking negatively.

"Hello, Mr. Alldredge," I said. "Nice tie."

"Well, come on in. Take a seat. How can I help . . . the two of you?" Mr. Alldredge asked as he slipped behind his desk.

Melissa looked a lot perkier than she had when we were out in the hall. "We want to talk to you about something that happened when we were taking the State Student Assessment Surveys."

Mr. Alldredge stopped smiling just like that and leaned forward in his chair. "What is it? What happened?"

The way the expression on his face changed so rapidly would have been neat if it hadn't been so scary.

Melissa's right knee started leaping up and down under her blue jeans. She leaned her hand against it and said, "Well, you see, during the English Survey we were given two essay questions to choose from. One of them we had seen before.

Mr. Borden had given it to us as an assignment. He was told he could use some old SSASies that were stored in the English Department so we could prepare for the test."

"You practiced the essay?" Mr. Alldredge broke in. "Is that what you're saying?"

His voice was tense, bordering on upset, and once you get to upset, the next stop is angry. I'd heard that tone of voice coming from a teacher a few times over the years, but Melissa hadn't. She began to sink down in her chair.

But she said yes without hesitating.

"Mr. Borden, you said? Excuse me for just a moment."

Melissa relaxed a little when Mr. Alldredge left the room, but I didn't because I guessed what was coming. A minute or two later we heard Mr. Alldredge's voice on the intercom.

"Mr. Borden, would you report to my office, please. Mr. Borden, report to my office."

Melissa gave this little shriek and kind of hopped once or twice on her chair. "Now what do we do?" she asked me.

"You said you had a plan," I reminded her.

"I never planned on Mr. Borden being here. I don't want to have to talk to him. What if he thinks I'm accusing him of cheating? You saw how he was when I asked him about the essay question in class."

"He did get kind of touchy," I recalled. "People get that way when they think they're being blamed for things. I can tell you that from personal experience."

"I'm not blaming him for anything!" Melissa insisted. "All

I want is for someone to fix this test problem and make everything all right."

All I wanted was to get out of there.

"I don't know what to say now," she said. "Nothing like this has ever happened to me before."

Something like this had happened to me, though. In fact, I was beginning to feel as if the old time and space continuum was totally twisted and I was being spun back to June. Mr. Alldredge's voice drifting out over the intercom, one of my teachers being called to the office, my backpack on the floor by my feet . . . all I needed was my father and a guy in a uniform to complete the scene.

As Melissa got more and more upset, I got calmer and calmer. Because, I realized, my life stunk so bad that this wasn't the worst mess I'd been in. The act of doing something different—getting hauled into the principal's office last year for carrying a concealed screwdriver—had made me a different person. I was used to things not going the way I expected them to now. All my plans had flaws. There was no point in going nuts and getting down on the whole world whenever things didn't go the way I wanted them to. I'd be nuts all the time. And then how could I keep my mind open for those surprising new opportunities to make the best of the many, many bad situations I was always in?

We could hear Mr. Alldredge speaking in the reception area. From the sound of his voice, he was walking back toward his office, and he wasn't alone. Melissa was teetering on the edge of her seat, as if at any second she would jump up and run for the window.

"You've got to control yourself," I whispered to her. "Don't—"

"Of course I'll control myself," she snapped at me, her voice shaking.

When Mr. Alldredge arrived, he had Mr. Borden with him. Mr. Borden sighed when he saw Melissa and shut the door behind him. He looked at me and his head drew back as if he'd had a little electric shock. I'm sure I was the last person he expected to see sitting in Mr. Alldredge's office next to Melissa Esposito.

Yeah, well, me too.

Mr. Alldredge sat down behind his desk, gave a big sigh that made the bottom of his mustache flutter a little bit, and said, "I know this is going to be awkward for all of us, but Melissa has told me some disturbing news. The charge she is making is so serious that I felt it was only fair to bring you in, Mr. Borden, so that you could hear and respond to it yourself."

Melissa had slid back in her seat and folded her hands in her lap. She was sitting up nice and straight. She looked pretty good. But when she opened her mouth to speak, the word "Charge?" came out with a squeak.

"You're accusing Mr. Borden of cheating," Mr. Alldredge explained.

Well, that was pretty much what *Happy Kid!* had predicted. For what good that was going to do me.

"Cheating?" Melissa croaked.

210

"If he helped you with the test, then he was cheating. Did he help you with the test?"

"No! Yes . . . ch-cheating?" Melissa said.

"I discussed this with Melissa in class," Mr. Borden said. "I thought I had reassured her about this issue. As far as cheating is concerned, how could I have done something like that? She took the test in her advisory with her advisory teacher. I wasn't even there."

"Not cheating. No, not cheating," was all Melissa managed to say.

"Assigning an essay question that later appeared on the SSASie?" Mr. Alldredge asked Mr. Borden. "It sounds a lot like cheating."

"I gave them the assignment weeks before this year's tests even arrived here at the school," Mr. Borden insisted. "It was one of many essays they wrote in September. I took all the topic questions from old SSASies."

Melissa couldn't say anything more than "ch—ch—ch."

I guessed she had pretty much finished saying whatever it was she had planned to say.

"The superintendent of schools is going to want to investigate this," Mr. Alldredge muttered. "And the school board. The PTO will have something to say about it, I'm sure. And then the newspapers." He looked over at me. "Accusations like this never go away, you know."

"Yeah, I know," I said. It would have been nice if he'd thought of that back in June when he was waving the student-parent handbook at my father and me.

Mr. Alldredge turned to Melissa then. "I want you to think very carefully about whether or not you want to do this. Mr. Borden might be removed from his classroom for at least a little while. You and your classmates may be questioned. I'm just telling you these things so you can make an informed decision. Whatever you decide to do, you will have my total support."

Sure she would.

Melissa turned toward me. Her eyes were filled with tears. She opened her mouth once as if she were going to say something, but didn't.

Hard as it was to believe, Melissa Esposito was speechless. If anyone was going to say anything now, it was going to have to be me.

"Melissa never accused Mr. Borden of cheating, Mr. Alldredge." I looked at Mr. Borden. "She didn't accuse you of cheating when she talked to you in class, either. You were the one who used that word. Melissa never *blamed* anybody for anything. She just wanted someone to fix this, to make it fair again for everybody. We're not talking about cheating at all. We're talking about an 'irregularity.' "

Both men looked at me as if I'd just said "constipated." Then Mr. Alldredge looked at Mr. Borden and said, "That's right."

"Melissa thinks it's wrong that our class had an advantage over the other kids. Mr. Borden didn't cheat, because he didn't know what questions would be on the test. What happened with the test was an accident, but if Melissa and I didn't do something to try to correct it, that wouldn't be an accident. That would be intentional. *We'd* be cheating now if we didn't try to fix this."

I got that part from Luke. He was going to be really excited when I told him I used his argument with the principal.

Then, just to wrap things up, I very carefully added, "No one is really to blame for any of this."

Mr. Borden looked over at Mr. Alldredge, who was gazing into space. Then Mr. Alldredge looked over at Mr. Borden and started to nod.

"That's right," he said. "There was no intent to do anything wrong so—no one's to blame!"

He looked at us and stood up, which, when a principal does it, is always a sign that a meeting is over. "Thank you both so much. You did the absolutely right thing by coming to tell me about this."

Mr. Borden patted Melissa on the back. "I don't want you to worry about class. I really respect what you did. I know it must have been hard."

I guess he didn't notice I was there.

Melissa sniffed and smiled and almost wiggled like a puppy she was so happy to have a teacher pleased with her.

"And you, Kyle, am I ever pleased to see you here backing up Melissa. Good work." Mr. Alldredge shook my hand.

He was about to open the door when he paused and said, "By the way, how many people know about the essay?"

I shot a quick look at Melissa out of the corner of my eye. She was biting her lip. Don't say anything, Melissa! I wanted to shout. He'll send his secret police out to collect them. They'll never be seen again.

"All the kids in our English class know. And some of them knew we were coming here today, too. Maybe four or five other kids know, and so do both my parents," Melissa told him.

She didn't give any names, and she made it seem as if a lot of people knew. Okay. I could see where she was going with that. There's safety in numbers. I wished I'd told more people.

"Let's try not to let it get all over the school until after we've decided what we should do about it," Mr. Alldredge suggested. "That way Mr. Borden can have some privacy while we're sorting things out."

Mr. Borden was going to get privacy. I got my picture in the paper.

"I really appreciate that, guys," Mr. Borden said, as if that would force us to agree to keep our mouths shut.

I could tell Mr. Alldredge didn't plan to do anything about that essay because he had that same look on his face that politicians and police officers get in Sci Fi Channel Original Movies when they're part of an alien plot to take over the world and are only pretending to help the main character stop it. It didn't matter to me. I said I would help Melissa, and I did. What happened afterward was none of my business.

But Melissa must watch the Sci Fi Channel, too (who knew?), because she had also figured out what was going on.

She was twitching and squirming and clearing her throat as if she had something to say.

"I have another question," she finally said just as Mr. Alldredge was saying good-bye to us. "How long will it take to sort this out?"

I couldn't believe she'd found the guts to start the discussion all over again, especially given how badly she'd done during the first round. Brad was right. She just didn't give up.

"It's hard to say," Mr. Alldredge said, just as my grandmother and Mr. Kowsz came walking into the office.

"You get everything worked out?" Mr. Kowsz asked us.

I took one look at Mr. Kowsz, the guy who made trouble for Mr. Alldredge over a gym teacher swearing at a seventh-grader, and saw one of those "surprising new opportunities" to make the best of a bad situation I found myself in.

"Oh, Mr. Alldredge," I said, turning back to him. "By the way? Mr. Kowsz knows about the essay, too."

The smiles left both Mr. Alldredge's and Mr. Borden's faces.

"I'm going to get right on it," Mr. Alldredge told Melissa. Then he tapped Mr. Borden's arm and said, "Come on back inside. I'd better call the school superintendent and tell him what happened."

"Does this mean you're done? What perfect timing," Nana said. Then she leaned toward me and whispered, "Tim and I are going to the home show at the civic center this weekend. We're going to look at tile for him to use on his lamp bases."

I heard way more about Mr. Kowsz than I wanted to on the ride home. He's fine in the dojang, but I don't know how I'd feel about him showing up with Nana for dinner on Sundays.

Nana left me off at home and went back to her office. I ran upstairs and picked up *Happy Kid!* I thought I deserved a new message. Maybe one that praised me instead of telling me what to do.

Share Your Cookies

Generous people form satisfying relationships. Give others your time and your attention and your knowledge. Pass this book on to someone who can use it.

I was going to have to give away my book?

CHAPTER 18

☹ ☺ ☺ 😐 ☹ ☹

Mr. Alldredge had asked us not to let the SSASie story get around school until after he'd decided what to do about it. But since the meeting ended with him calling the school superintendent, I figured, Well, he's decided. So when Luke phoned me that night to see what happened, I told him. Melissa must have felt the same way, because Jamie and Beth said that when they called her, she told them, too. That was how the information spread throughout the seventh grade before we went to bed.

By the time we got to advisory the next morning, Mrs. Haag had heard and wanted all the details. Jamie and Beth squealed through the whole story and asked us over and over again if we hadn't just wanted to, like, die when Mr. Alldredge called Mr. Borden to his office.

"Everyone's talking about you," Luke told me in art.

Which was true. All the talk was about me standing up for the regular students in the school and not letting the kids in accelerated English get away with taking an easier test. I started thinking very positively. I was positive Chelsea was going to see what a heroic and noble thing I'd done and like me more for it.

"Everyone is really impressed," Luke went on.

"Ah, all Kyle had to do was threaten to kick Borden's ass," Jake scoffed.

"Yeah, that would have gone over well," I said.

My triumph would have been more . . . triumphant . . . if I could have reached into my backpack to sneak a peek at *Happy Kid!* and found a better message than "Share Your Cookies." I didn't want to give away *Happy Kid!* What if I gave it away to someone who didn't "get" the book? What if the person laughed at me, dumped the book somewhere, and never used it? Giving it away would be kind of a waste then, wouldn't it? To say nothing of how little I'd enjoy the being-laughed-at part.

But I looked in *Happy Kid!* whenever I had a chance, and there was no change. The book was determined to go to someone else.

Before social studies started, a bunch of A-kids came up to ask me how Mr. Borden liked getting called to the office. All the time I was talking with them, I could see Chelsea watching from across the room. Chelsea could see that I was with A-kids, that they wanted to talk with me. Even Ms. Cannon wanted to talk with me. I was handing in some papers at the end of the class, and she whispered, "Good for you, Kyle. You cannot imagine how much underhanded activity goes on at the university where I'm working on my Ph.D. No one does a thing about it. I could tell you stories . . ."

She looked as if she was getting wound up to tell one right then, but the bell rang and I was saved.

Then I got to English.

At first when I saw that Mr. Borden wasn't there, I was relieved. I'd been worried about what kind of mood he'd be in. Melissa, however, didn't look anywhere near as pleased as I felt. She looked suspicious. And in her typical Melissa way, she went right up to the substitute and asked where Mr. Borden was.

The sub looked as if she'd graduated from college just that morning. She got all flustered and said, "I'm not supposed to talk about it."

"Well," Melissa insisted, "how long will he be gone?"

"I think only a few days. Just until they can schedule some kind of a test. That's all I was told."

It was enough.

Immediately, the room felt different. People looked around at each other. There was sighing and grumbling. Somebody muttered "I hope you're happy" to no one in particular, though I'm certain he meant for Melissa and me to hear it. Melissa must have thought so, too. She went to her seat and slowly sat down. She kept her back straight and her head up as she opened her copy of the book we were reading. As if anybody could read under those circumstances.

Never in my whole life had I been so happy to leave a

class. And I've been happy to leave a *lot* of classes. I thought I'd made my escape when I heard someone calling my name.

I turned around and saw Chelsea coming toward me. I started to smile. Chelsea had called my name. She was coming to me. At last, we were going to talk. Everything was going to be all right.

She just kept coming and coming, every tall, blond inch of her.

She got right up close to me and hissed, "You moron. That test was my best shot at getting into that special English class next year. I just barely made it into accelerated English in sixth grade. I need a good SSASie score, and I would have had one with that essay I wrote. But now who knows what will happen? I could end up in a regular English class with everyone else next year. How will that look?"

Here, at last, was my first big conversation with Chelsea. I had never thought about what she might look like up close and yelling. It turned out she wasn't anywhere near as pretty as she was when she was sitting quietly on the other side of a classroom. I was also surprised to notice that she could have used a little mouthwash.

"And what do you think is going to happen to you when you take that test over?" Chelsea went on. "You think *you're* going to do well enough to get into that ninth-grade English class without having practiced the essay?"

I sure hoped so. Because if Chelsea ended up in a regular English class next year and she was still this unhappy about it, I didn't want to be there with her.

"Well," I said, "I do very well on the SSASies as a general rule—and without having to cheat, either."

"Get out of my way!" Chelsea ordered.

I almost yelled, Make me! But I knew she was five ranks above me in taekwondo and probably could.

During lunch I was back to being the man of the hour. Also during health and living. By seventh period, though, I didn't want to talk about Mr. Alldredge, Mr. Borden, or essay questions anymore. I wasn't used to having people "Yo, Kyle" me and tell me I was the man and things like that. It was wearing me out.

I was out in the hall before science class started with Luke and a couple kids when Jake came along. Everyone but Luke took off to avoid him. Jake stopped in front of me.

"Are you *still* going on about that lousy meeting? You didn't do anything but talk. Now, if you had kicked Borden's ass, I'd be able to see what the big deal is about. But since you didn't—"

"Jeez, Jake, would you lay off with Mr. Borden's ass?" I snapped. "I didn't kick it, and I'm not going to. So give it up."

Both of us kind of gasped and almost seemed to jump away from each other. It was obvious why I did. I'd just yelled at Jake Rogers. But why would he gasp and jump back from me?

Because he was afraid of me, I realized. Ever since the state trooper had come for me, Jake had been treating me as if I were like him—someone to be afraid of. My first thought was, How nice. The guy in my class most likely to end up in juvie detention sees me as a scary person. *There's* something I can be proud of. My second thought was . . . *Wait just a minute here.* The guy in my class most likely to end up in juvie detention sees *me* as a scary person. This is a good thing!

I have definitely become such a positive kind of guy.

"Hey, back off, okay?" Jake finally said, his arms raised up in front of him. "I was just making a suggestion."

"Don't make it again," I said, feeling braver than I probably should have.

Jake told me I could kiss his ass and went into our science classroom. Since names can't hurt you the way Jake Rogers's big meaty fists can, I was very pleased with the way that turned out. But Luke said I'd better keep going to my taekwondo class because I might need to be able to do more than kick someday.

Being heroic and noble, at least to people who are not A-kids, is all very nice, but did it make my homework load any easier? No, it did not. Tuesday afternoon, things didn't go any faster than they ever had. I just managed to get everything done in time to get into my dobok.

When we arrived at the dojang, Mr. Kowsz—Tim—was coming out of Mr. Goldman's office. We all bowed to one another, and he said, "Mr. Goldman and I were just talking about you, Kyle. Do you know when your braces are coming off?"

"I don't think they are, sir."

Tim laughed. "If you make green belt by the end of March—and you might, even though you have to make yellow belt first—it will be time for you to start wearing full gear when we're sparring. That includes a mouth guard. Oh, don't worry. You won't be the first person to spar in braces."

"I could make green belt by the end of March?" I asked.

"It's up to Mr. Goldman. He decides when you're ready to test for the next level. But, honestly, the only thing that could slow you down is your control problem. He may want you to wait to move on until you've learned to control yourself better so you don't get hurt or hurt someone else. Other than that, you're golden."

"So, am I doing well because I'm golden or doing poorly because I'm not controlling myself?" I asked him.

Tim thought a minute. "You choose," he finally answered.

"*I'd* choose that I was doing well," Luke said happily as we followed Tim into the training area.

Luke is an incredibly positive person. I didn't usually notice that kind of thing, but I still had to give *Happy Kid!* away to someone—someone, the book said, who could use it. I didn't know who that would be, but I was sure it wouldn't be Luke.

I was able to forget about that problem while I warmed up because I was so busy watching Chelsea put her foot in her hand and do that leg-stretching thing she always does in front of the mirror. She did look fantastic. But I could tell from the expression on her face that she thought so, too.

After Mr. Goldman had us line up and practice punching and kicking, he said, "Gear up! Yellow and white belts— tonight you can borrow chest protection from the school for sparring practice."

Tim helped the lower-ranked students find vests that fit us and showed us how to lace them up. Then the class formed two lines so that we could turn and face a partner.

"We're doing control drills tonight, people," Mr. Goldman called.

I looked over at Tim, who nodded at me while Mr. Goldman said, "First round, just punching. Light contact only. Just touch the vest. And I want to hear a shout when you make contact."

For sixty seconds my partner and I just sort of tapped at each other's vests and shouted. Then Mr. Goldman called a thirty-second rest. We did another round together and then the lines shifted so we could switch partners.

I can do this, I thought. The control thing isn't that hard.

We did another round of punching and then a round of kicking. Controlling kicks is harder than controlling punches, and I started to get tired. When Mr. Goldman told us to punch *and* kick, still only tapping our opponent's vest, I got confused because how was I supposed to know when to punch and when to kick?

Then there was all the yelling we were all doing.

I was gasping for breath when we switched again, and I found myself standing across from Chelsea.

"Fighting stance!" Mr. Goldman called.

We both stood there staring at each other, our hands up, one leg back.

"Go!"

Chelsea went right after me with a roundhouse kick that she turned into some kind of spin and backwards thing that I hadn't learned how to do yet. Her foot hit me so hard, I staggered back while my head bobbed forward.

"Chelsea! Light contact!" Mr. Goldman shouted.

I started moving away to try to avoid her. Which actually seemed to encourage her. She'd stop attacking me for a few seconds to sort of laugh and bounce up and down on her bare toes. Then she'd come after me again.

Suddenly, Tim was behind me. Chelsea backed off when he showed up, and he pulled me out of line.

"You have to use kicks to keep her away. Use your legs so she can't get close to you," he said in a low voice, keeping his eye on Chelsea to make sure she was too far away to hear.

"She can kick better than I can," I objected. "She's better than I am."

"She knows more than you do right now, but no way is she better than you are. Make her think you're going to punch, then catch her off guard with a kick. To avoid being hit, she'll stay away from you." He pushed me toward Chelsea. "Do it," he said.

Do what? I thought as Chelsea put her hands up into guard position and started bouncing again. I'd already for-

225

gotten what Tim had told me to do, and even if I hadn't, how could I have done all that in the time we had left in this round?

"Faster, Kyle," Tim called from somewhere behind me. "You have to *move*."

Move where? Move what?

I pulled my right arm back as if I were getting ready to throw a punch. Chelsea moved just enough to avoid my fist. I brought my right knee up, then quickly rotated on my left foot so that when I was ready to kick, I was turned sideways to her. My foot went forward into a very nice roundhouse kick, if I do say so myself. She would have at least been knocked to her right a few steps if I'd hit her full on the side. But I didn't. I slowed down so I just brushed Chelsea's vest while I shouted, "Hiya!"

She backed up and I chased her, this time brushing her with a roundhouse kick with my left foot. She was on to me by then. She moved in closer so that she'd be too close for me to get my foot up. She got me with two hard punches to the chest, but then I was able to get far enough away to do the roundhouse thing again.

When the round was over, Mr. Goldman made Chelsea do twenty push-ups in front of everybody for ignoring his instructions about using light contact.

Maybe Chelsea could use a book like *Happy Kid!* I thought as we were all leaving the dojang later. But I didn't think I wanted to hear what she'd have to say after I gave it to her and told her what it was.

That was the problem with giving the book away. The people who needed *Happy Kid!* the most were going to be really unpleasant when I explained what it was and why I was handing it over to them. The people who would be nice about it didn't need the book.

Happy Kid! had screamed my name at my mother while she was walking by it. Maybe if I just left it somewhere, it would scream a name to someone passing by.

I packed the book in my backpack the next morning. I had to be careful about it because I didn't want it falling out in front of the wrong person again, but I wanted to be able to get a hold of it in a hurry if I found a good place to leave it.

Melissa was sitting by herself at her desk when I got to advisory. I went up to her and said, "What if they give us two worse questions than the ones that were on the original test?"

Melissa shrugged. "There's a fifty-fifty chance they will."

"You're not even worried about taking that test, are you? You're dead certain you'll do well enough to get into that ninth-grade English class next year."

"Well, Kyle, we have been taking the SSASies for years. We ought to have a pretty good idea how we'll do on them," she pointed out. "Haven't you even looked at your scores?"

"Of course I have. And they're fine. They are just fine," I said.

"Well, then, what are you worried about?"

"I don't know if they're fine enough to get me into an A-kid class," I admitted.

"They must have been fine enough in fifth grade to get you into A-kid English and social studies here at Bert P. Trotts," Melissa said.

There was a long pause before I broke down and said, "What?"

Melissa closed her eyes and sighed. "We went through all this in social studies one day. The schools use the SSASies as placement tests for students who are moving from one school to another in the same town. The scores we got on the SSASies in fifth grade were used to decide which classes we'd be in when we got to sixth grade here."

I lost some self-control for just a moment and exclaimed, "I'm an A-kid?"

"Haven't we talked about this?" Melissa asked. "Why did you think you were in 'A-kid' English and social studies, anyway? Because of some kind of mistake?"

I just laughed as if she'd made a really funny joke. Fortunately, Melissa didn't seem to actually expect me to answer her question. She went on to ask another. "Why do you care about getting into one of the high school classes next year, anyway? You don't seem to like the accelerated classes you're in now. Oh, wait. It's because of Chelsea, isn't it?"

She knew? Did everyone know?

"Well, it wasn't a secret," Melissa said. "She called you a moron in the hallway yesterday. Of course you've got to get into that English class now so you can prove to everybody you're not one." She shook her head. "Name-calling—it's not right."

I thought I heard something. Maybe it was just the beginning of an idea.

"Remember how you said you were going to tell everyone
I had that book *Happy Kid!* if I didn't go see Mr. Alldredge
with you? Would you have really done that?"

"Of course I would have," Melissa said huffily. "When I say
I'll do something, I do it."

"No, you wouldn't have. You wouldn't have done it because it wouldn't have been right to use something private
you knew about another person against him. Just like it never
occurred to you to choose the second essay topic when we
took the English SSASie so you'd get a better score. You don't
do things like that."

"I needed someone to go with me, and I asked every person in that class before I asked you. *Everyone.* I just don't get
it. How can people know that something is wrong and refuse
to do something about it? How can they stand themselves?"

"Some people think that a person can be *too* right," I suggested.

"And that's their excuse for not doing the right thing? Ha!
They're just scared. They're scared people will treat them the
way they treat me whenever I have to do something like reporting Mr. Borden's mistake by myself because they won't.
But you know what? They really like that I do those things for
them. It means they don't have to do them. Oh, it's always
the same. They laugh and make jokes about me, maybe they
stop talking to me for a while, but then they get over it and
everything is back to normal."

"Ah, Melissa, maybe when the other kids laugh and make jokes about you, it's not just because you're right," I suggested. Helpfully.

"What else could it be?"

I had an idea. Or maybe I just heard something screaming Melissa's name.

I pulled *Happy Kid!* out of my backpack and handed it to her. "Here. You really should read this."

Melissa sneered. "I don't need a stupid self-help book."

"Oh, believe me, Melissa, you do. I showed you how it works," I said as I forced *Happy Kid!* into her hands. "Let it fall open and read whatever you find there."

Melissa hardly had to do anything. The book practically popped open as soon as she touched it. We both looked down to see what it had to say.